He Was In The Midst Of A Complicated Business Deal, And He Had Slept With The Opposing Bidder.

What made matters worse was that she had no idea who he was. He had deceived her.

He needed to tell Meredith who he was.

How had he lost control? Was it hearing that he had been her only lover?

The truth was, he had been attracted to Meredith from the moment he saw her at her party. He had hoped that time would have lessened his reaction to her. But it hadn't.

It seemed to have made it worse.

She had opened up to him, trusting him to see her vulnerable. And he had encouraged it. In spite of himself, he wanted her to trust him. To care about him.

He was a fool. Because once Meredith found out who he was, she would want nothing more than to get away from him.

Dear Reader,

As expected, Silhouette Desire has loads of passionate, powerful and provocative love stories for you this month. Our DYNASTIES: THE DANFORTHS continuity is winding to a close with the penultimate title, *Terms of Surrender,* by Shirley Rogers. A long-lost Danforth heir may just have been found—and heavens, is this prominent family in for a big surprise! And talk about steamy secrets, Peggy Moreland is back with *Sins of a Tanner,* a stellar finale to her series THE TANNERS OF TEXAS.

If it's scandalous behavior you're looking for, look no farther than *For Services Rendered* by Anne Marie Winston. This MANTALK book—the series that offers stories strictly from the hero's point of view—has a fabulous hero who does the heroine a very special favor. Hmmmm. And Alexandra Sellers is back in Desire with a fresh installment of her SONS OF THE DESERT series. *Sheikh's Castaway* will give you plenty of sweet (and naughty) dreams.

Even more shocking situations pop up in Linda Conrad's sensual *Between Strangers.* Imagine if you were stuck on the side of the road during a blizzard and a sexy cowboy offered *you* shelter from the storm…. (Hello, are you still with me?) Rounding out the month is Margaret Allison's *Principles and Pleasures,* a daring romp between a workaholic heroine and a man she doesn't know is actually her archenemy.

So settle in for some sensual, scandalous love stories…and enjoy every moment!

Melissa Jeglinski

Melissa Jeglinski
Senior Editor, Silhouette Desire

Please address questions and book requests to:
Silhouette Reader Service
U.S.: 3010 Walden Ave., P.O. Box 1325, Buffalo, NY 14269
Canadian: P.O. Box 609, Fort Erie, Ont. L2A 5X3

Principles and Pleasures

MARGARET ALLISON

Silhouette® Desire

Published by Silhouette Books
America's Publisher of Contemporary Romance

SILHOUETTE BOOKS

ISBN 0-373-76620-3

PRINCIPLES AND PLEASURES

Visit Silhouette Books at www.eHarlequin.com

Printed in U.S.A.

Books by Margaret Allison

Silhouette Desire

At Any Price #1584
Principles and Pleasures #1620

MARGARET ALLISON

was raised in the suburbs of Detroit, Michigan, and received a B.A. in political science from the University of Michigan. A former marketing executive, she has also worked as a model and actress. She is the author of several novels and is happy to return to the world of romance after taking some time off to care for her young children. Margaret currently divides her time between her computer, the washing machine and the grocery store. She loves to hear from readers. Please write to her c/o Silhouette Books, 233 Broadway, Suite 1001, New York, NY 10279, or visit her Web site at margaretallison.com.

One

Until Meredith saw Josh Adams, she had been thinking that this year's holiday party might just be her mother's most successful ever. Elaborate ice sculptures decorated her family's impressive foyer. Hundreds of votive candles were placed strategically, winding up staircases and layered across tables. Furniture had been moved to make room for the live spruce trees decorated with tiny gold lights and crystal icicles. And, as usual, all of Aspen high society had turned out to dance, sip champagne and eat caviar.

Meredith watched as he moved through the crowd, smiling and shaking hands. She had not seen Josh in more than ten years, but he had not aged a day. Curly brown hair, smoky-gray eyes and a sexy just-rolled-out-of-bed grin. It was as if he had never left for Europe, as if crashing the party of an ex-lover with whom he had not spoken in years was the most natural thing in the world.

Although, she reminded herself, ex-lover was a generous term for what they were to each other. It had been one night, nothing more.

But, oh, what a night.

Focus, she reminded herself. She could not afford to be distracted by childhood crushes.

Still, she couldn't help but wonder what had brought him back after all this time. Josh had been a friend of her younger sister, Carly, and Carly had not mentioned him in years. The last Meredith had heard was that he had moved to Europe to continue his career as a ski instructor to the wealthy.

Ignore him, she told herself.

She weaved her way through the horde of people, doing her best to play the role of hostess. It was a difficult chore for someone who was so distracted, even more difficult for one who preferred spending her evenings behind her desk, reviewing the latest financials. As CEO of Cartwright Enterprises, once one of the largest conglomerates in the country, Meredith had a difficult job. The company had been hemorrhaging money, driven into financial ruin by her stepfather. An addicted gambler, he had embezzled millions of the company's dollars before taking his own life. The stock had fallen drastically, taking their family fortune along with it.

As Meredith greeted a woman she barely knew with the standard cheek kiss, she found herself glancing over her shoulder, looking for Josh. Why was he here? As far as she knew, he had not been invited. She would have remembered if Josh's name had been on the invitation list.

But then again, if Carly had decided to invite him at the last minute, she would not have bothered to mention it to Meredith. After all, why would she? Carly knew nothing about Meredith's night with Josh. Meredith had never found the right moment to admit the truth: she had seduced the greatest womanizer Aspen had ever seen.

Carly, she knew, would have been shocked. As would all of Aspen. The Goody Two-shoes nerd falling for the playboy. No one had any idea of how Meredith had grown up longing for Josh, of how many parties Meredith had spent hiding at the top of the banister, watching Josh flirt with all of the girls.

She drained her glass of champagne. What was the matter with her? After all, she had not seen or spoken with him since the day they'd made love, all those years ago. Josh had left for Europe shortly after, where she assumed he still lived.

It was the party, Meredith realized. Her nervous brain had kicked into third gear, tossing up everything and anyone who had ever made her feel uncomfortable. She glanced at her watch. It was nearly eleven o'clock. She had to endure several more hours.

Never one to indulge in gaiety or frivolity for the sake of it, Meredith could not remember the last time she had been to an event that wasn't business-related. Her whole life could be defined by one word: work. She had spent her college years with her nose to the grindstone and it had paid off. She had graduated magna cum laude from Harvard and had gone to work in her family's Denver, Colorado-based company. She'd worked her way up and had been the obvious choice for CEO when her stepfather died. The shareholders had voted her in as president of Cartwright Enterprises at the age of twenty-nine.

Since then she had worked long and hard to try to save their failing company from financial ruin.

Ironically, however, it was not Meredith who was saving their company but Carly.

Carly, although she had a title and office at Cartwright Enterprises, had never shown up for a day of work. But she had shown remarkable sense in love.

Meredith had long had her eye on a product called Durasnow, an artificial snow that stayed fresh in temperatures above freezing. Meredith had had little hope of acquiring the rights. After all, Durasnow was a product that could revolutionize the skiing industry. But Carly's engagement had given her a leg up on the competition. Suddenly, Meredith had a family connection, and when she offered an all-stock deal, the Durans had seemed excited. Everything was finally moving on track.

"Meredith," said her mother. "Have you seen Carly?" Viera Cartwright raised an eyebrow, indicating her displeasure.

"No. Why? What did she do?" Meredith asked. Although Carly was almost thirty, her mother still treated her as a child. There was something about Carly that made people want to take care of her. An almost delicate and vulnerable air that made one think she was incapable of taking care of herself.

"Her friend Josh is here."

Meredith's heart quickened.

"You remember him," her mother said, misinterpreting Meredith's silence. "Your old skiing instructor."

"Yes," Meredith replied as casually as she could. "I know. I saw him."

"Well? Who invited him?" Viera asked unhappily.

"Does it matter?"

Her mother bit her lip. "Carly was just mentioning him the other day."

"So? They were friends for a long time."

Viera's voice dropped to a stage whisper. "She was asking me if I ever had any regrets when I got married."

"Regrets?" Meredith whispered back. "What did she mean by that?"

"She said the only regret she had was that she had never slept with Josh Adams."

Meredith inhaled sharply. Her sister had a crush on Josh Adams? "She's getting married in a couple of weeks!"

"You don't think I know that? I just ordered five thousand dollars' worth of white orchids."

"But she loves Mark."

"Of course she does. But she's Carly. And Mark is out of town until Friday."

Carly had always had her pick of the men in Aspen. She was known for her fickle heart, falling in and out of love as easily as some changed hairstyles. But it seemed that with Mark Duran, she had finally found the man of her dreams. The handsome, serious surgeon had won her heart and had Carly changing her ways. Or so Meredith had hoped.

"Where is she?" Meredith asked.

"I don't know," Viera replied. "And I don't see Josh, either."

"I wonder why he came back," Meredith said, concerned. "He's been living in Europe for years."

"Yes. Quite a coincidence," her mother said sarcastically.

"What do you mean?"

Viera sighed. "I just hope Carly hasn't contacted him or done something foolish."

Meredith gave up looking for Carly and began searching for her sister's future in-laws, the guests of honor. If not for them and the impending purchase of Durasnow, the prudent Meredith would have called off her mother's expensive holiday party. After all, they no longer had the funds to support such an extravagant lifestyle. But Meredith knew that a cancellation would stir rumors of financial hardship. And so, with the prospect of good fortune and wanting to squash any rumors of family turmoil, Meredith had allowed her mother to hire, buy and pay for the best of the best.

And now, it seemed, it was all a waste. All because of Josh Adams.

For once Meredith wished she'd told her sister the truth about what had happened that night on the mountain with Josh. Perhaps if Carly knew that Meredith and Josh had a history, Carly wouldn't be lusting after him.

A waiter walked past carrying a trayful of filled champagne glasses. Meredith did a quick count. Twelve glasses at ten dollars a pop. One hundred and twenty dollars on the tray alone. And at that moment, there were at least twenty trays being passed around. Not to mention the trays of fresh shrimp, the lobster tails on the buffet... the elaborate French desserts. The thought of the amount of money involved was overwhelming. It was enough to make Meredith set her glass down and take another. She downed the champagne and turned back to her mother.

"Where are the Durans?" Meredith asked, referring to her sister's future in-laws. Her mother glanced upward, toward the second-floor balcony. Meredith followed with her eyes. The Durans were standing by themselves. If the scowls on their faces were any indication, they were not enjoying the party.

"I'll take care of them," Meredith said, handing her mother her empty glass. "You look for Carly."

Meredith pushed her way through the crowd. She grabbed hold of her long black satin gown and climbed the steps, two at a time. She wished she had worn what she'd wanted, instead of allowing her mother and sister to talk her into this ridiculous frock. She would've been much more comfortable in her black satin pants and shirt. "Wayne…Cassie," Meredith said, approaching the Durans. "I was just talking to the Morrows about the quality of Durasnow—"

"Meredith," Mr. Duran said, cutting her off. He pointed toward the dance floor. "Who the hell is that?"

Meredith turned. Carly stood under the ornamental lights in the corner of the room. And she was not alone.

Josh looked every bit as entranced by Carly as she was by him.

"Oh," she said with a forced laugh. "That man? The one dancing with Carly? He's our former ski instructor. We grew up with him. He's practically like a brother to us."

"I never danced with my sister that way," Wayne said.

"Ha-ha," Meredith laughed stiffly, trying to fight the panic building inside. "Josh lives in Europe."

"Well, he's certainly here now, isn't he?" Wayne snapped.

"He certainly is," Meredith said. "If you'll excuse me, I absolutely must go say hello."

How could Carly do to this to her? Do this to herself?

If Mark heard about the way she was cavorting with a known womanizer...

She forced herself to take a breath. They were dancing. And that was all....

Carly leaned over and kissed Josh's neck.

Meredith did a half jog the rest of the way. "Carly!" said Meredith, practically jumping in between them. "My goodness! Here you are. Your future-in-laws are looking for you."

Meredith focused her attention solely on her sister. She did not acknowledge Josh. She could not look at him, for fear a mere look would give her away. *Ignore him,* she reminded herself.

"I'm busy," Carly said. Her words were slurred just enough for Meredith to recognize that her sister had been enjoying the champagne. This was trouble. Plain and simple.

"Hello, Meredith."

At the sound of Josh's voice, Meredith felt a tickle at the base of her spine. She shook it off. She reminded herself she no longer felt anything for the man to whom she had lost her virginity. It was a childhood crush, that's all. She was long over him.

"Hello, Josh," Meredith managed to say, glancing at him as casually as she could. Suddenly she felt like giggling for no reason whatsoever except that Josh Adams was standing beside her. She was back in high school. She was the nerd talking to the most popular boy in town.

Meredith glanced toward the balcony. The Durans were watching them. Cassie Duran leaned over and whispered in her husband's ear while shaking her head in disapproval. Meredith snapped out of her reverie.

"Carly," she said. "I need to speak with you."

"I'm busy," Carly said.

"I'm afraid I have to insist," Meredith said, taking her sister's arm. She attempted to give Josh a casual smile. "Nice to see you again, Josh."

"Meet me in the gazebo in ten minutes," Carly said to Josh. She turned back toward Meredith and yanked her arm away. "What is so important that it couldn't wait?"

Meredith said, "Upstairs."

Viera met them at the landing and whisked them into the second-floor library.

Viera slammed the door behind them. "What are you doing?" Viera asked Carly. Her voice was shrill and accusatory. "The other day when you were talking about Josh, I didn't honestly think you were serious. I didn't think you would contact him and arrange to meet him while your fiancé was out of town."

"Calm down, Mother. I wasn't."

"What do you mean?" Meredith asked.

"I mean, Josh just showed up. Out of the blue. Isn't that weird?" Carly leaned back in the chair, smiling contentedly.

"Have you been drinking?" Meredith asked, knowing her sister rarely drank.

"A little champagne," Carly said, pinching her fingers together.

"Carly," said her mother. "Think of Mark. What's he going to say when his parents tell him about you cavorting with another man?"

"It's not just any man. It's Josh." She focused her innocent eyes on Meredith. "Meredith, tell her. Tell her how special Josh is."

"Me?" Meredith swallowed. "What makes you think I...well..."

"It doesn't make any difference anyway," Carly said, sounding like a spoiled child. "It's nobody's business but mine."

"That's where you're wrong," Viera said calmly. "If you don't marry Mark..."

"We'll lose the precious Durasnow contract," Carly said. "Well, I am marrying him. But I have one more wild oat to sow first."

"Carly!" Viera gasped.

Meredith and her mother exchanged a glance. Meredith held her breath. This was terrible. Awful. Her sister was going to fool around with Josh? The man to whom she had lost her virginity? The only man she had ever slept with?

She needed to admit the truth to her sister right now. To confess her history with Josh. It's just that...well, what did it matter anyway? It was a long time ago. One night. She doubted Josh even remembered.

"It's none of your business if I—" Carly stood. "If I—" She held her hand to her mouth and swallowed.

"Carly?" Meredith asked. "Are you all right?"

"I—excuse me..." With one hand over her mouth and one on her stomach, Carly ran into the bathroom.

"This is terrible," Viera said. "Her whole future. Ruined. It's the curse. The curse of the Cartwright women."

Meredith knew what her mother was referring to. The Cartwright women were known for their poor choices in husbands. Meredith and Carly often joked about the infamous men in their family. Their great-grandfather had died in the arms of another woman, as had their grandfather. Viera's first husband, Meredith's father, was also a notorious playboy. He died of a heart attack just like his father and grandfather, while making love to a woman who was not his wife. Viera's second husband, Carly's father, was not a playboy but a thief. After bilking millions of dollars out of his wife's company, he killed himself shortly after the board discovered his crime.

"She loves Mark. She'll marry him," Meredith said. She could not bear the thought of her sister losing Mark. Carly had chosen a man unlike her father or her grandfather. Mark Duran was sweet, earnest and madly in love with her.

"Careful," her mother said, "you sound like a romantic. Practical Meredith…at least I'll never have to worry about you."

"Why not?" Meredith said.

"Because you're not like your sister, giving your heart away to this man or that man."

"You're saying you don't have to worry about me because I don't have a boyfriend?"

"You've never had a boyfriend. Not that there's anything wrong with that," her mother said. "You just prefer to be alone than date some of the eligible bachelors that have expressed interest."

"What eligible bachelors?" Meredith asked. It was true that she had never had a boyfriend, but she wasn't avoiding men. She dated…occasionally.

"Frank…for one," she said, mentioning a local dentist with whom Meredith had shared several dinners.

"I'm not interested in him. No chemistry."

"See?"

"I don't want to go out with just anyone. After all, I'm busy. I have a lot of responsibility."

"Of course, dear." But Meredith could tell from her mother's voice she did not understand.

"I'm one of the only women running a conglomerate," Meredith continued.

"Of course, dear," her mother repeated.

"And it's not as if I turn men down," she said. "I can't remember when I was asked out last."

"You're smart, Meredith," her mother said. "Most women your age are rushing around, caring for their husbands, their children. You just have to worry about yourself."

"Right," Meredith said, rather uncertainly.

"Especially now, during the holiday season," Viera continued. "Most women your age are busy with parties and presents. But you don't have to bother yourself with any of that. I'm sure this Christmas you'll be at your office, dealing with business as usual."

Carly opened the bathroom door. She made her way over to the couch and lay down. "I'm sick," she said.

"Too much champagne and men," her mother said.

"Speaking of which—" Carly touched a hand to her forehead "—Josh is waiting for me." She turned toward Meredith and said, "He's in the gazebo. Tell him that I couldn't make it, but I'll see him tomorrow."

"Me?" Meredith asked. She did not want to see Josh alone. What if he mentioned their night together? It was too awkward. "Maybe you should go," Meredith said to her mother.

"Absolutely not," Viera said. "I'm going to find the Durans and try to smooth things over. Besides, I really don't care if he stands there all night. Let him freeze his—''

''Mother!'' Carly said. ''Please, stop talking. My head is spinning.'' She grabbed Meredith's hand and held it. ''You'll go?''

Meredith looked at her sister. She always had a terrible time refusing her anything. ''Okay,'' she said. Taking a breath for confidence, Meredith headed toward the door. Out of the corner of her eye, she could've sworn she saw her sister mouth something to her mother. But when she turned back, Viera was frowning and Carly had her eyes closed.

''Go on,'' her mother said. ''And hurry back.''

Meredith walked out of the room. She tried to swallow the sadness welling in her throat. It had pained her to hear her mother sum up her life like that. But she knew Viera was not trying to be cruel. After all, it was the truth. Meredith had no social life. And it was looking as though she never would. Whereas Carly always had too many men to choose from, Meredith never had any.

But her mother was wrong to assume she liked her situation. She had not planned on being the girl never asked to dance. During college, she had tried to change. Tried to be more like Carly. And that was how she'd ended up with Josh.

Meredith blushed as she remembered how it had all come about. She had harbored a secret crush on Josh all through high school. Several years older than her, he was a gifted ski instructor. He dated socialites, girls like her sister, beautiful and charming. Meredith, in contrast, was tall and awkward, with brown hair, brown eyes and glasses. She was the type of girl that boys would choose as a study partner, not a dinner date.

Meredith had left Colorado for college on the East coast, hoping to forget about Josh. But her social life had not improved. Among her friends she was known as the "virgin." All they ever talked about was men and sex. "It's like plunging into freezing cold water," one of them said. "It's a little weird at first, but then you get used to it."

"Just do it," another advised her. "Don't be so picky. Men are going to start thinking there's something wrong with you."

But Meredith wanted her first time to be perfect. She wanted her first lover to be kind and considerate. Skilled and confident.

Finally, as she'd entered her senior year of college, Meredith had become tired of waiting. If she was ever going to lose her virginity, she was going to have to take action herself. But there was only one man with whom she wanted to make love.

Josh.

She'd spent months planning a seduction. She'd tried to make herself into the kind of woman Josh might find attractive. She'd gotten contact lenses, lost weight, had a professional makeover. And she'd made a plan. Over Thanksgiving break she would hire Josh to take her to the top of Bear Mountain. A one-day trip, she knew there was a halfway house that was stocked with supplies for skiers stuck on the mountain. She would feign a sprained ankle, forcing them to stop at the cabin.

Everything had gone flawlessly.

Meredith had lost her virginity in a romantic, memorable night of passion. Although it had been everything Meredith had dreamed, she had not been happy.

In fact, the morning after, when she'd awakened

wrapped in Josh's strong arms, she'd been overcome with remorse. What had she done? She'd tried to turn herself into someone that she was not, only to bed a man who would never be hers. Angry with herself, she'd promised she would never again compromise herself for another man.

And so she had gone to the opposite extreme. She no longer bothered putting on flirtatious airs or worrying about makeup or hair. She was who she was. A corporate executive.

Meredith went through the back of the house, trying to avoid the crowd. She grabbed the big, thick, down coat that her sister said made her look like a stuffed Eskimo, put on her warm snow boots and stepped outside.

Meredith spent most of her time in Denver, where Cartwright Enterprises had their corporate offices. But nights like this made her miss Aspen. It was a beautiful evening. The air was cold and clean, the sky lit by thousands of sparkling stars. She glanced across the yard, toward the gazebo, which was lit by tiny white lights. She could see Josh standing, his hands in his pockets, waiting.

She swallowed. *Make it quick,* she told herself. *Just tell him that Carly can't make it and be on your way. You don't have to make conversation. You don't have to stay and talk...*

"Meredith?" Josh smiled as he stepped closer. "This is a surprise."

Meredith stopped outside the gazebo and said, "Carly couldn't make it."

"Oh?"

"She's sick. Too much..." She paused. It was not

Josh's business why her sister was ill. "Food poisoning."

"Oh," he said. "I hope it wasn't the crab dip. I helped myself to that, too."

"No," she said. She stood there, her feet rooted to the ground.

"So," Josh said. "It's been a long time."

"Yep," she replied. Yep? She had commandeered the takeover of corporations. So why was she acting like a naive little schoolgirl who didn't know how to speak?

She thought she saw a twinkle in his eye. A smile crept up the corners of his lips as he said, "How are you, Princess?"

It was a voice that could melt butter. Normally, Meredith bristled whenever anyone referred to her in a chauvinistic manner. No one she knew would have ever dared call her "Princess." But then again, no one called her "dear," "sweetheart" or "baby," either. Pet names were too informal for a woman like Meredith.

"Good," Meredith said. She patted the front of her coat, a nervous habit. "How have you been?"

"Fine," he said. "Great. And you?"

This was disastrous. Meredith had never developed the skills of making small talk. If it wasn't related to business, she was as awkward as the girl she once was. "Wonderful, thank you."

"You look great," he said.

Once again she could feel the blush burn her cheeks. So she asked, "Why are you here?"

"Carly asked me to meet her here."

"No. I mean, why are you back in town? I'd heard you were in Europe."

Josh sat on the bench that ran around the inside of the

gazebo. "And I heard you were the head of Cartwright Enterprises."

Meredith looked into his deep gray eyes and was immediately transported down memory lane. He was once again the boy who had touched her so knowingly, once again the man to whom she had given her virginity. Their one night alone had made her think that sex was a magnificent, ground-shaking experience. How wrong she had been. The few kisses she had received since then had been awkward and wet.

"Yes," she said.

She had heard from him several times after their night together, but had been too embarrassed to respond. She'd known the deal before she'd slept with him. Josh Adams was not a one-woman man.

"How are things going for you?" he asked in the same sexy voice.

"Good," she said. "Great." It was a lie and anyone but Josh would know it. Everyone had heard the story: Cartwright Enterprises, once one of the most influential conglomerates in the world, was fighting for survival. If it wasn't for Durasnow, she would have been anticipating filing bankruptcy papers.

"Really," he said, raising his eyebrows. She couldn't tell if he was questioning her or if he was just making conversation.

"So," she said. She entered the gazebo, moving a little closer. "Sounds like fun. Living in Europe and all."

"I guess," he said. "I still miss some of the people from around here."

Like Carly? "Surely you've made other connections

by now," she said, touching her index finger to her pounding forehead. "Are you married?"

He laughed. "No."

"Is that funny?"

He hesitated for a moment, looking at her. "Still the same Meredith," he said. She doubted he meant it as a compliment.

She clasped her hands in front of her. *No,* she thought. *Looks too awkward.* She unclasped her hands. She stood still, her hands stiff at her sides.

He smiled again. "What about you?"

She shook her head. *Hands beside me, hands beside me...* Why did he keep looking at her like that? She cleared her throat. "I heard you were working at a ski resort in Switzerland."

"More or less," he said.

More or less. She wouldn't have expected him to maintain a full-time job. She knew his type. Play by day and by night. She guessed he was still keeping the same hours he'd kept in Colorado. Saving his energy for his women. Only now Josh was probably dating women half his age.

He said, "I'm flattered you kept tabs on me."

Meredith felt as if she was being baited. "I wasn't keeping tabs," she replied. "I must've heard Carly mention it."

He nodded toward the bench. "Have a seat," he said. "I'd like to talk to you."

But she didn't move. She'd had enough small talk. "You never said what brought you back to Aspen."

"Business."

What kind of business would a ski instructor have? But still, that did not mean he had returned for Carly.

In fact, the idea of Josh Adams returning to confess his love for Carly was preposterous. He and Carly had been friends, nothing more. What would inspire him to come back...

"Meredith?" He was looking at her curiously. "Are you all right?"

She had to laugh. Josh would, too, if he knew what she and her mother had been thinking. "This is going to sound ridiculous, but I thought for a moment that your reason for returning might have something to do with Carly."

Josh wasn't smiling. "It does."

Meredith felt a lump lodge in her throat. It was not jealousy, she told herself quickly. She could not be jealous that Josh had come back for her sister and not her. After all, he and Carly were friends. She and Josh were...well, they were nothing.

"She's getting married, you know," she said.

"Yes," he said. "I know." His face darkened. He met her gaze directly, as if daring her. "I wanted to..."

But Meredith didn't let him finish. She read his reaction as confirmation of her fears. "Leave her alone," she blurted.

"What?"

"She's happy. You'll just confuse her."

"I don't know what you're talking about." He stood and walked toward her.

She held his eyes. "I think you do." She could see the muscles in his jaw tighten. She knew she was making him angry but she couldn't stop herself.

Meredith stepped back. "Do you want money? Is that it?"

"Is that what you think?" He stepped closer to her.

So close, he was almost touching her. His eyes glared at her, burning a hole.

"Because she's not quite the heiress these days. In fact, if she doesn't get married, she may not have any money at all."

"I see," he said.

Meredith was no longer the naive little schoolgirl. She was once again the head of Cartwright Enterprises. Past history aside, she was not about to let some playboy ruin her future. "So we understand each other?" she said to Josh.

"I understand you perfectly, yes. You're saying that Carly has to marry to save your ass."

"I beg your pardon?"

He glanced toward the house. His breath was white in the frosty air. "I'm touched by how important your sister's happiness is to you."

His words hung in the air. He was being sarcastic.

"She loves Mark."

"So what are you so worried about? Surely she has some time for an old friend," he said.

"Because she's…she's Carly. And Mark may not be so understanding."

"It sounds like perhaps they shouldn't be getting married."

"I'm asking you as a…as a friend. Please go."

"I'm sorry, Meredith. As a friend," he said, as if he found the word distasteful, "I can't do that."

This was the man she dreamed about? The one with whom she compared all others? "I'm sorry, too," she said. She spun on her heels and began to walk away.

"Meredith," said Josh.

She stopped. But she did not turn around.

"Please tell Carly I'll see her tomorrow."

She stood still for a moment and then walked slowly back to the house, her head held high.

How dare she?

Josh sat on the bench, taking a few moments to compose himself. He had heard the rumors. Meredith Cartwright was so desperate to save her company that she had sold her sister. And, unfortunately, it appeared to be true. Meredith wanted Carly to marry Mark Duran so that she could get her hands on Durasnow.

And she thought that he, Josh, might interrupt the deal. She was right, of course. But he had not come back to steal Carly. He had done something much worse.

He had returned for Durasnow.

He had wanted Durasnow for years—he'd been the first to express an interest. But once Carly and Mark became engaged, the Durans had informed him that they'd felt obligated to entertain bids from Cartwright Enterprises. When Josh had read that Meredith had publicly declared her intention to buy Durasnow, he'd known the Durans had been less than honest. The writing was on the wall: the Durans would play Josh against Meredith, bidding up the price. In the end, neither would win. So Josh had come back to broker a deal. Perhaps he and Meredith could join forces and buy Durasnow together.

But Meredith was right in a way. He had come tonight because he'd wanted to see Carly. After all, he had not spoken with Meredith since their night together. He had tried to contact her several times but she'd never returned his phone calls. But her reputation was well-known. She was a stubbornly independent woman. So he had hoped that perhaps Carly might act as go-between, brokering a deal between Europrize and Cartwright.

Meredith, obviously, had no idea who he was. She assumed he was still the same playboy that had left Aspen.

The mere thought of his former lifestyle was enough to put a smile on his face. How things had changed.

It had not been an easy transition. Shortly after his night with Meredith, his aunt died. He had been surprised to learn that she, a waitress of seemingly meager means, had managed to save fifty thousand dollars. The instructions she'd left in her will had been simple. *Make me proud.* His friends had encouraged him to use the money for travel, to continue his life uninterrupted. But he'd had no intention of frivolously spending the money for which his aunt had worked.

His aunt had given him a new chance at life, a chance to remake himself. And he preferred not to have any reminders of the boy he once was.

Not that his life growing up had been all bad. Without the experience he'd gained, he never would have started his business. He knew his old friends had been surprised to learn that he'd been able to utilize the skills he'd learned in his former life and turn them into a multi-million dollar business that had made him one of the richest men in Europe.

His company, Europrize, had developed several interactive video games that had been sold to a major technology company, leaving him with more than enough money to buy out the richest men in Aspen. But he was just getting started. His newest venture, buying and renovating ski resorts, was already bringing in revenues.

But their earning capability was limited to the season. If he could stretch out the season a month or so on each side, especially if his was the only ski resort open, the business would boom.

Which is why he wanted Durasnow. He had been following the Duran company for a while, his eye on their product. He'd approached them about buying the rights and they had seemed interested. But Wayne Duran reminded him of many of the men he had known from Aspen. A seemingly friendly but ultimately untrustworthy guy. Although Josh had been promised the rights, he'd had nothing in writing. He hadn't been surprised to learn that a major conglomerate had suddenly gotten involved.

But he had been surprised to learn it was Cartwright Enterprises. It seemed odd to be up against a family he had known for years. He and Carly had once been good friends, but through the years they had lost touch, corresponding less and less. And Meredith…he had not spoken with her since their night together.

His fingers tightened around the edge of the bench as he thought of her. Meredith had not been like the other women in Aspen. She'd been quiet and intellectual, a girl who seemed to always have her nose in a book. Whereas Carly had been with a different boy each week, Meredith had never seemed to go out at all.

Most of the girls had just ignored her and the guys hadn't been much better. But they were not just being cruel. Meredith had a way of speaking to people that was extremely off-putting. She'd handled her peers as if she were a queen dealing with mere commoners. Her behavior had become a running joke between his friends, who had dubbed her "Princess," short for Ice Princess.

It wasn't that she was a typical snob, thinking that she was better than everyone else because of her family money. Not at all. Meredith, with her mismatched outfits and tights with holes, cared little about money. Meredith was an intellectual snob.

She'd always been the smartest person in the room, and she'd known it. Still, there was something about her he'd found appealing. He realized later that in an odd way he related to Meredith. Meredith had suffered the loss of a parent and had had a troubled relationship with the man who had taken her father's place. Josh's own family history was similar. His mother had died when he was young and his father had married a girl just out of high school when Josh was eleven. He had not gotten along with his young stepmother. His father later divorced her and married another—a woman who was even worse than the first. The situation had gotten so bad that Josh had moved in with his mother's sister.

Although he'd enjoyed living with his aunt, she'd never really been his parent. In a town where family and money determined one's success, Josh had had neither. He may not have looked the outcast that Meredith was, but inside, he'd felt like her.

One night he'd attended a party and stumbled upon Meredith sequestered in the library. She'd been sitting at a desk, reading intently. She'd removed her thick-lensed glasses, and her long, curly hair—usually pulled tightly back—had been loose around her shoulders. In that moment he'd thought her the most beautiful woman he had ever seen.

She had looked up at him and smiled, a rare thing for Meredith. Encouraged, he'd struck up a conversation. It was as if she was a different person. They'd spoken for hours, rambling about everything from Thoreau to the state of the ski slopes. He'd felt a connection between them, an understanding.

But he'd been called away by friends and, although Meredith had promised to wait for him, she had gone by the time he returned. Afterward, he'd thought of little else: the feeling of excitement, the anticipation he'd felt at seeing her again. The next day he'd arrived at the lodge early, fully aware that Meredith was to be his student in a trek down Lost Mountain. But his anticipation was for naught. When Meredith arrived, her figure hidden beneath layers of clothing, her beautiful eyes once again covered by her thick, tinted lenses she'd acted as if nothing had changed. Whatever spell had possessed her the previous evening had been broken. She'd obviously had no interest in him.

He'd attempted to put her out of his mind and, for the most part, was successful. Sure, he'd feel a mild sting of curiosity—a what-if?—whenever her name was mentioned, but that was all. Life went on.

During the next five years, he interacted with Meredith briefly, with nothing really happening. Then things changed one Thanksgiving weekend when Meredith returned from her expensive Eastern college looking as though she'd enrolled in beauty school. His friends, most of whom had never even noticed her before, had suddenly taken an interest in her. But Meredith had had her sights set on him.

She'd hired him for a private lesson. She'd chosen Bear Mountain, one of the most difficult courses in Aspen. Accessible only by helicopter, it was a private and expensive run. It was so difficult that the owners kept a stocked halfway house for those who were either too tired to make it down the mountain or got caught in one of the blizzard-like snowstorms that engulfed it several times a week.

He had given Meredith private lessons before, but none that had required packing an overnight bag. And although Josh had found himself in sticky situations before with amorous female students, he'd never suspected Meredith's intentions.

Not even when she'd hurt her ankle and insisted on going to the cabin. Although he'd known her injury was not severe, he'd been more than happy to acquiesce. He'd helped her back to the cabin, relishing the feel of her as she'd leaned against him. When she'd told him to wait before calling for assistance, he still hadn't suspected anything untoward. Because by then, he'd been so smitten with her that he'd been barely able to think.

Sitting across from her in that cabin, he'd been tongue-tied. He'd realized that he'd had nothing to say to a woman like Meredith, so educated and intelligent. And for the first time in his life, he'd cared.

Fortunately, Meredith hadn't seemed to mind. She'd appeared relaxed and at ease, seemingly metamorphosing into a completely different, warm and flirtatious person. He'd lost track of time and, before he'd realized, it had been too late to call for help. They'd had no choice but to spend the night in the cabin on the mountain. As he'd watched Meredith limp around the room, he'd realized that she had switched legs, that she'd been faking her sprain. For whatever reason, she had wanted to be alone with him as much as he had wanted to be with her.

And when Meredith had moved to sit beside him, he

hadn't hesitated. He'd done what he had wanted to do since that night in the library. He'd kissed her.

She'd been a surprising lover. Passionate and daring, wildly responsive. So much so that, until he'd entered her, it had never occurred to him that she'd be a virgin. He had pulled out immediately, afraid of hurting her. But she had insisted and he had continued, albeit at a more gentle pace.

Knowing that he'd been the first to touch her had only increased his desire. He'd wanted to consume her, to keep her beside him always. He'd wanted her to be his and his alone forever.

But when the dawn broke, the feelings that had engulfed him had been replaced by more familiar ones. A dull, throbbing discomfort, a reminder of a need to be alone. A desire to stay single and unattached.

Fortunately, Meredith's ankle had miraculously healed. After an awkward morning with stilted, uneven spurts of conversation, they'd skied down the mountain in silence. When they'd parted at the lodge, he'd made the promise he made to every woman who shared his bed. *I'll call you.*

It had taken him several days, but he had called and been somewhat annoyed when she hadn't called him back. In fact, he'd begun to feel desperate when she hadn't returned any of his calls over the next several days. Suddenly, he no longer cared if he spoke with her again and it hurt him that she hadn't felt the same.

The truth had been bitter and unavoidable. "She thinks she's too good for me," he had told his aunt a week later.

His aunt had not beaten around the bush. "She is."

As hard as it was to hear those words, he'd known

his aunt had been right. How could he even have hoped to woo someone like Meredith? He'd been an uneducated playboy, a man whose only interests were skiing and women.

"At least, right now," his aunt had added. "But who knows what the future holds. Perhaps you will prove her wrong."

His encounter with Meredith became a turning point in his life. For the first time he'd started to think about the boy he was and the man he wanted to be. When his aunt had died and left him the money, she'd given him the means. He'd always had the will.

He had often thought about seeing Meredith again and wondered what it might be like. He had to admit, laying eyes on her tonight, after all these years, had taken his breath away. When he'd last seen her, she'd still been a girl about to come into her own. She was now a woman, poised and confident, radiantly beautiful. But from what he had heard, looks were deceiving. Meredith had a reputation as one of the most ruthless chief executives in the business.

So ruthless that she was willing to trade her sister's happiness for artificial snow. Although he had a hard time believing that Carly would let herself be manipulated like that, he still found the entire deal suspicious. He did not trust the Durans and had no intention of getting into a secret bidding war with Meredith. He had been involved in those before and had found himself the victim of the winner's curse more than once. The price would become so inflated, the final tally seldom reflected the true value. But from what he had seen tonight, Meredith Cartwright was not a woman who would listen to reason.

So he would continue on his course and attempt to reach Meredith through Carly. Although she was not as brilliant as Meredith, she was still an astute and energetic individual. He would try to win Carly over by explaining the situation and having her act as an intermediary with her sister. He would also make it clear to Carly that she did not have to marry Mark for Cartwright to win the rights. If only Meredith would agree, they could share the company.

Once again he thought about how Meredith had offered him money to leave Carly alone. What would make her think he had come back to woo a woman with whom he had not spoken in years? Besides, he had never been romantically interested in Carly. She was and always would be, in his eyes at least, a less impressive version of her older sister. He would never be able to look at Carly without remembering the night Meredith had finally quenched his thirst.

He stood and began to pace. He would not go back to the party. But he would return tomorrow. Meredith could not intimidate or manipulate him. She may not realize it yet, but she had met her match in Josh Adams.

Two

The dining room table was at least thirty feet long, big enough to seat forty people. Meredith sat at the head of the table, across from her mother. Carly sat in the middle, exactly halfway in between.

Meredith did not like this table, nor did she care for the room. It was too ostentatious and showy. But her mother had grown up dining in this room. And although there were no longer servants to tend to the fire in the fireplace or to bring out steaming plates of food, her mother still insisted that they all drink their morning coffee beneath a one hundred and fifty pound chandelier.

Meredith glanced at her mother who had just finished telling the story of how the decorated Christmas tree in the living room had crashed to the ground, causing havoc and tearing the Ritter sisters' gowns.

"It's those men who installed it," Viera said. "I told

them they weren't putting the trees in the stands correctly, but they didn't listen.'' She sighed deeply and dramatically as she focused her attention on the newspaper spread out in front of her. ''It's so hard to find a man you can trust.''

''Speaking of men you can trust,'' Carly interrupted, turning toward Meredith. ''You're going to make me ask, aren't you?''

''What do you mean?'' Meredith asked, sipping her coffee.

''What happened with Josh? Did you talk to him?''

''Yes.''

''And?'' Viera asked as she pushed her bifocals lower on her nose so that she could see Meredith.

''And nothing.'' She shrugged and took another sip.

Carly and Viera glanced at each other. ''You were certainly gone a long time,'' Viera said. ''I didn't see you all night.''

''Well, I wasn't with Josh,'' Meredith said, setting down her cup. ''I came back and went to bed.''

''Why is he back in Aspen?'' Carly asked.

''I don't know. But I think it has something to do with you.'' Meredith felt a slight ping of jealousy. *Ignore it,* she told herself. *And it will go away.*

''With me?''

Meredith nodded. ''He said he wanted to see you. In fact, he said he would see you today.''

''Really?'' Carly smiled and sighed dreamily. ''He looked so handsome, didn't he?''

''I didn't notice,'' Meredith said quickly.

''There's just something about him. A charisma. It's like a sexual fire or something.''

''Sexual fire?'' Meredith asked.

"A spark. The way his eyes twinkle."

Meredith paused, remembering the eyes that had stared so deeply at her. She agreed with her sister. Josh's eyes were the kind that seemed to bore right through you.

"And the way he smells. It's so woodsy and manly-like."

Meredith remembered how she had awoken from her night with Josh, how she had felt surrounded by his musky scent. She was surprised that her sister would mention something so personal about Josh. Carly was speaking like his lover, not like his friend.

"And he's so confident and self-assured—"

"Have you heard from Mark?" Meredith interrupted.

"I guess," Carly said.

"What do you mean, you guess?" Viera asked. "Either you have or you haven't."

"What difference does it make? All I can think about is Josh."

Meredith leaned forward, certain that she had misunderstood. This was her horrible imagination playing tricks on her.

Her mother glared at Carly. "I've got four hundred people coming to your wedding in two weeks. I suggest you stop thinking about Josh and start focusing on your future husband."

"I can't stop thinking about him." Carly glanced away. "I have to see Josh."

"What would Mark say if he heard you talking like this?" Viera exclaimed.

Carly shrugged. "I think he would think the same thing I'm thinking. If I'm so tempted by another man, then maybe we shouldn't get married."

"That's the most ridiculous thing I've ever heard!" her mother practically screeched.

"Mother—" Meredith began, trying to calm Viera.

"If," her mother interrupted, looking at Carly, "you care nothing for me, think about your sister. What's going to happen to the deal with the Durans if you break their son's heart? Your sister could lose her job."

On the assumption that Meredith would be purchasing Durasnow, her company's stock had been rising. And so had the board's confidence in her. If this deal fell through, the company might still survive, but Meredith's tenure as CEO would be over.

"You're right, Mother." Carly sighed deeply. "What's wrong with me?"

Meredith couldn't speak. What *was* wrong with her?

Josh's obvious charm aside, Meredith couldn't understand why Carly would want to jeopardize what she had with Mark. They seemed so happy together. Meredith had often wished she would be so lucky as to find someone who cared about her as much as Mark cared about Carly.

Carly put her head in her hands. "It's the curse," she cried. "I finally meet a good guy, a guy that I love and who loves me. It's all going to be ruined. Just because of Josh."

Perhaps her sister was right, Meredith thought. Perhaps it was just the Cartwright women's knack for romantic self-destruction that was leading her astray.

Carly focused her wet, blue eyes on Meredith and said, "You're the only one who can help me."

"Me?" Meredith asked, surprised. "What can I do?"

"Keep him away from me." Carly threw her head in her hands, her long, curly blond hair falling forward.

Meredith thought back to the previous evening when she had offered Josh money to leave Carly alone. The defiant fire in his eyes had been unmistakable. Meredith shook her head. "I can't keep him away. If you don't want to see him, you have to tell him yourself."

"I can't. I'm afraid if I see him...if I'm alone with him...well..."

"You'll pick up where you left off?" It was Viera who spoke.

Meredith held her breath, waiting for her sister's answer. She had always assumed that nothing romantic had ever transpired between Carly and Josh. But then again, would Carly have told her if it had?

"Left off?" Her sister appeared startled by the question. "We've never even dated. We were always just friends. I mean, I've dated some cads, but Josh was almost too much of one even for me. I knew so many girls that were hurt by him."

Meredith exhaled. At least Carly had not slept with him.

"And this is the man with whom you can't stand to be alone?" Viera asked slowly, as if she was also having trouble grasping the problem.

Carly's eyes settled on Meredith. "Distract him, Meredith. Just until Mark gets back."

"What? How?"

"Hire him to give you skiing lessons. Ask him to take you to Bear Mountain. That's at least a solid day. By the time you get back, Mark should be home. I'll be safe."

"You better be 'safe,'" Viera said, making quotation marks in the air with her fingers. "We've got five hundred people with invitations and gifts expecting a wedding.''

Meredith raised her eyebrow. "A minute ago there were four hundred."

"Replies are coming in as we speak," Viera said defensively. "It's the event of the season."

Meredith shook her head. "I don't know." She sighed. "If Carly is having so many second thoughts then maybe…" Maybe she shouldn't get married. As much as she hated the idea of losing the contract with Durasnow, she couldn't stand the thought of her sister being in a loveless marriage. "Maybe…" Meredith began. *Just say it.* She glanced at her sister. "Maybe your marriage to Mark is not meant to be…"

"It *is* meant to be," Carly said.

"Excuse me?"

"I just need a little help avoiding the curse."

Meredith shook her head, not convinced. "What if you get married and start feeling this way about someone else…"

"I won't. It's just Josh. I think he could tempt any woman to misbehave."

Meredith sighed. She couldn't argue with that.

"Sometimes matters of the heart don't make sense, Meredith," her mother added, glancing at Carly.

The doorbell rang, its chime echoing through the empty house. Carly stood and moved to the window to peek out. She ran back to Meredith and clutched her arm. "It's Josh," she said. "Ask him to take you to Bear Mountain or something. Please."

But Meredith couldn't bear the thought of seeing Josh again, not to mention asking him on a trip. "I have to work. I'm supposed to go to New York today."

Viera stood and said, "If your sister is seen with Josh, you may not have a job to worry about."

"Just for a day or so. Until Mark gets back."

"Carly—" Meredith began.

Carly interrupted. "If you won't do it for me, do it for your…"

"Country?" Viera suggested.

"I was going to say company," Carly said, "but whatever works."

Meredith hesitated.

"A day, Meredith," Carly said. "Please?"

"All right," she said, standing. "One day." She walked away, certain she had just made a deal with the devil. No good would come of this. No good at all.

Josh stood with his back to the Cartwright door, admiring the view of the mountains. At times he missed those long days with nothing better to do than ski. He had gone from one extreme to the other. From ski bum to corporate entrepreneur. There has to be, he thought, a happy alternative.

Hearing the door open, he turned, expecting to see one of the Cartwright servants. Instead, Meredith stood in front of him, her thick, dark hair loose around her shoulders. She was dressed casually, in a tight-fitting turtleneck and jeans. He couldn't help but notice the outfit clung to her like a second skin.

He felt a warmth stir inside him. The once uncertain girl had become a captivating swan who was not only aware of, but also relished the change.

She looked at him and nodded.

Josh had long prided himself on his ability to recognize his opponent's strengths and weaknesses. He had an innate sense of people. So far, at least, his instincts had not led him astray.

And his instincts told him one thing. Whatever was about to come out of her mouth would be interesting.

Meredith focused her bewitching brown eyes on him and smiled. "Please come in. Carly is waiting for you."

He heard Carly gasp from the other room. "I'm sick, Meredith!"

"Don't be ridiculous. It's just Josh. He just wants to say hello." Meredith turned back toward him. "I'm sure she's well enough to welcome an old friend…"

Carly burst past them, covering her mouth. Viera followed close behind.

"I'm afraid Carly is sick with the stomach flu," Mrs. Cartwright said, hurrying after Carly but pausing at the base of the stairs to flash Josh her famous, white-toothed smile. "Josh," she said, as if she suddenly had all the time in the world. "Carly's obviously not in any shape to entertain an old friend. You'll have to settle for Meredith."

Viera nodded toward her daughter. "Why don't you invite Josh in? There's coffee in the dining room," she added as she made her way up the stairs.

"What was that?" he asked.

Meredith shrugged her delicate shoulders. He thought he could see the hint of a smile. "I guess Carly's not as well as I thought." She paused and focused her oval eyes on him. He had the feeling she was summing him up, deciding what to do with him. "I'm afraid this flu is a nasty one."

"Perhaps I should come back later." He caught her eyes and held them. Was this a ploy to keep him from speaking to Carly about her fiancé's company?

No. He had seen Carly with his own eyes. She may not have the flu but she was obviously ill. Still, he couldn't help but tease Meredith. If she thought so little of him that she believed he had returned to seduce her sister, especially after what he and Meredith had shared, then so be it. "As you know," he continued, "I'm very anxious to see her."

"Of course," she said.

If he was annoying her, she didn't show it. He shrugged. "Perhaps tomorrow. I'm free all day so—"

"You're free all day?" she interrupted.

"All day."

She hesitated, and glanced once more at the top of the stairs, as if waiting for Carly to appear. Finally she said, "Good."

"Good?"

"I was hoping you'd be free."

"You were?" Just the night before, she had been ready to run him out of town.

Once again, she smiled. It looked stiff and practiced, the kind of smile one saved for photographs. "Why don't you come in?"

"All right," he heard himself say.

"Can I get you some of the coffee Mother offered? Although," she added conspiratorially, "I should warn you it's a little weak and lukewarm."

"No thanks." He followed her into the dining room, his eyes taking in the seductive swing of her hips as she moved. "Although it does sound enticing."

She offered him a seat then sat across the table from him.

Josh was struck by the quiet. It was the strange quiet of empty, cavernous spaces. Slightly forced, as in a museum. And that's just what this house looks like, Josh thought, glancing around. A stern, slightly faded museum. Meant to be admired, not lived in.

Meredith smiled. The nervousness had disappeared. Once again she seemed confident and self-assured. And why wouldn't she be? How could a woman who had grown up in a castle with the world at her feet be anything else?

"I wanted to apologize for last night. I was…out of line."

"Yes," Josh said.

She laughed. "It was all so ridiculous. Too much champagne will do that, I'm afraid."

Funny, but she hadn't seemed intoxicated. He had the feeling Meredith Cartwright did not lose control of herself very often. But still, that did not excuse her behavior. Nor did it explain why she would consider him such a threat to her sister's marriage that she was willing to pay him to leave town.

"Anyway…" Once again she paused. Her eyes held him as she said, "I was wondering if you still give lessons."

"What kinds of lessons?" He raised his eyebrows. He thought he could see a slight blush on her high, exotic cheekbones.

"I was curious as to whether you'd be interested in giving me a ski lesson. I've been meaning to take some time off and go skiing, but it's been a while."

He hesitated, unsure of how to respond. Was she serious? "You want me to take you skiing?"

She nodded.

Did she really not know who he was? Did she assume

that he was still the good-for-nothing playboy instructor she'd once known? "Meredith," he began. "I'm not…"

A black cell phone on the table began to ring. "Excuse me," she said, answering her phone.

Josh watched her, confused. Perhaps, he thought, this was a ploy. Perhaps she really did know he was also bidding on Durasnow. Perhaps this was her way of getting him to tell her the truth.

"Tell me again," he heard Meredith say. She paled. Whatever the news, it was not good. "I thought it was ours. What do you mean, they're accepting other bids?"

So, he thought, the jig was finally up. He'd told the Durans last night that they had a responsibility to tell Meredith that they were also negotiating with him. Apparently they had gotten the message.

"Find out who this phantom company is. I don't care how much money they have. They are not getting Durasnow," she said coldly. "Over my dead body." She hesitated, listening to the voice on the other end of the line. "How thoughtful of them," she said after a while. It was a voice that could chill even the warmest of hearts. "And now I want you to make our position clear," she continued. "Under no circumstance will we negotiate with anyone. I want this product and I'm going to get it." She snapped the phone shut.

So she was not willing to negotiate. She was still every bit as headstrong as she was beautiful. But her arrogance was going to cost her Durasnow. "Problems?" he said.

"Nothing I can't handle." She took a minute to regain her composure. "Anyway," she said, focusing her attention on him once more. "I was thinking that perhaps you could take me to Bear Mountain tomorrow."

"Bear Mountain?" he repeated, surprised. What was going on?

He must have appeared reticent because she said, "The standard day rate for a top instructor is five hundred dollars. I'll give you six."

"Six hundred dollars?" he asked. "To take you to Bear Mountain...again?" Meredith's eyes shifted. She remembers, he thought. She knows damn well that Bear Mountain is where we made love. So what is she doing? Is this some sort of corporate strategy? Or is this her weird way of apologizing for bad behavior ten years ago? Or perhaps she's feeling lonely. Did she think she could buy companionship?

"I haven't been since the last time you took me," she continued, meeting his eyes. "But if you don't feel up to the challenge..."

And then he didn't care what game Meredith was playing. He was ready for whatever she had in mind. "You're on."

Three

————

"**I** just don't think this is a good idea," Meredith said one more time to her mother as she threw some items into her backpack for today's lesson with Josh.

"It's the *only* idea. You've got to keep Josh away from Carly. What if Mark hears about her gallivanting around town with a known playboy just weeks before their wedding?"

"Well, I'm not looking forward to it," Meredith said. *Maybe,* she thought, *if I say it enough I might actually start to believe it.*

"Meredith, try to enjoy yourself. After all, he's gorgeous, single and charming."

"This is not a pleasure trip," Meredith said. But for a moment, her mind flashed on the past. She remembered the way it had felt when Josh had kissed her, how he had leaned forward and touched his lips to hers, his hand pressed against her lower back, pulling her up against him....

"Meredith?"

Meredith swallowed and zipped up her pack. It did not matter what had happened between them. Josh had come back for Carly, not her. It was Carly he remembered.

Not that she blamed him. Carly was charming and beautiful. Meredith had never seen herself as a beauty and although she tried to be pleasant, she knew most people found her aloof. It wasn't that she didn't care about other people, she did. It was just that social situations made her uncomfortable. And the truth of the matter was, she had never learned how to make small talk. Growing up, she had few friends, instead finding companionship in her books.

She had grown up the good girl. Never causing problems, never making waves. She had worked harder, longer, faster than anyone else. And it had cost her. After all, who wanted to be friends with Goody Two-shoes? Who wanted to date a woman who was known for being unapproachable?

"I don't know, Mom," she said. "If we have to go to such extremes..."

"What's so extreme? You're keeping a nuisance out of Carly's hair," Viera told her. "And it's just until Mark returns. Then everything will be back to normal."

Meredith glanced toward the window. In the distance she could see Bear Mountain.

"All right," she finally conceded. After all, it was one day. What could happen in one day?

Hours later Meredith was bundled up, waiting beside her car at the heliport for Josh. Most of the chief executives Meredith knew were driven around in limousines, but thinking them a ridiculous waste of expense, she would take a taxi or drive her own car just like everyone else.

Limousines hadn't been the only executive perk Meredith had eliminated during her tenure at Cartwright. In her efforts to cut costs she had taken away almost all of the executive benefits. Her actions had done much to improve the morale at Cartwright and the board was encouraged. Meredith may have grown up with a silver spoon, but it had not affected her work ethic. She was known as a down-to-earth boss, a woman who wouldn't ask anything of an employee she wouldn't ask of herself.

"Sit inside and keep warm," the pilot said, motioning toward his helicopter. "I'm sure Mr. Adams will be here any moment."

Meredith checked her watch and saw that she had been here almost an hour. Not that she was surprised that Josh was keeping her waiting. She guessed it was intentional. After all, when she'd called to confirm her lesson he'd been cold and short, as if she were inconveniencing him. It had taken all her willpower to not call the whole thing off.

Was he purposely trying to anger her? she wondered, getting into the helicopter. Or perhaps he had simply lost track of time. After all, it didn't take much to distract Josh. Any attractive woman would do.

It was not difficult to imagine Josh still in bed, making mad, passionate love to a woman.

The mere thought was enough to make her heart sink. After all, Josh was the only man she had ever slept with.

It was pathetic. Thirty-two, and only one lover to her credit.

Her lack of sexual experience was not something she had planned. True, she had always been different from other girls her age. While they'd played house or written notes to boys, she'd studied the works of Plato and memorized the strategies of Machiavelli. It wasn't that she hadn't wanted to get married one day, it was just that she'd considered other things more important. And besides, if her mother was any example, marriage was no ticket to happiness.

She hadn't eliminated men from her life. She dated occasionally. But her life was busy and already so full that she had to like someone an awful lot if she was to make time for them. And there had been no one that special.

Pulling her jacket tighter around her, she thought, Perhaps he's not coming.

Her heart dropped. She felt an actual pang of despair.

Horrified, she was reminded once again that a part of her actually looked forward to this trip. But why? Did she think their history might be repeated? Did she *want* history to be repeated?

Suddenly she saw a dirty blue Jeep pull in, skis sticking out of its open roof. Most people would consider it too cold to drive an open vehicle, but the cold didn't seem to bother Josh. He wasn't even wearing a hat. It appeared as if her suspicions were correct. Josh looked as though he had just rolled out of bed. His brown hair was tousled and his face sported a day's beard. He was wearing a black ski jacket, jeans and hiking boots. He raised his sunglasses and smiled at her. She stepped out of the car and into the helicopter.

Within a second, she felt a blast of cold air as the door opened. His backpack landed in her lap. "Toss this in the back for me, will ya?" he asked.

She unbuckled her seat belt and shoved the pack next to hers in the back.

"Something wrong?" he asked, catching her eye as he jumped into the helicopter.

"Why would you think that? Just because I've been waiting almost an hour?" She knew she sounded shrill, but she couldn't help herself. Damn, she thought. Talk about playing it cool. She sounded like a jealous girlfriend.

"Sorry for the delay. I had a business matter."

"What was her name?" she asked quietly, the question out before she could stop herself.

"Excuse me?" he said, leaning closer.

She looked into his liquid gray eyes with the full belief that just moments earlier he had been staring at another woman. Damn, he was handsome. The growth and messy hair just made him look more rugged and sexy. "Nothing," she said weakly.

"All right then," he said cheerfully to the pilot. "Let's go."

As the helicopter lifted off, Meredith felt her heart jump into her throat. Once again she was not sure if it was the feeling of leaving mother earth or if it was the idea of the trip itself. She was going off with a man she barely knew…a man she hadn't seen in years. A man to whom she had lost her virginity.

"What are you thinking about?" he asked.

Meredith flipped open her phone. "Work."

Josh opened up a bag of raw carrots. He offered her

one. She shook her head and held up her cell phone as she turned away, yearning for privacy.

She dialed her office and had to practically scream above the noise of the helicopter. "What's going on?"

Her assistant told her that despite their best efforts, they had been unable to determine the identity of the company bidding for Durasnow.

Meredith forgot about Josh and forgot about being hundreds of feet in the air. Her mind was focused on the problems at work. "Why not?" she asked, unable to hide her frustration. It was not entirely directed at her assistant, but she couldn't help but wonder if she would've found the answer had she done the research herself.

"It is absolutely imperative you find out who it is," she yelled into the phone before slamming it shut.

"Problems?" Josh asked. He tucked the empty carrot bag into his pocket and adjusted his gloves.

"Nothing I can't handle."

"I'm a pretty good listener," he said. "In case you feel like talking..."

"No," she said quickly. "No thanks. I don't think you'd find it interesting."

"You might be surprised. Besides, I thought I heard something about snow..."

"Josh," she said tartly, "it's a product, not a weather report."

He raised an eyebrow and she thought she saw the hint of a smile forming at the corners of his mouth. Turning away again and flipping her phone open again, she glanced out the window as the helicopter flew over the side of a cliff. They were sailing into the air, thousands of feet above the ground. Bear Mountain was straight ahead, looming ominously in front of them.

What was she doing?

She could've kicked herself for being away at this crucial moment. How had she allowed herself to be talked into this? Wouldn't it have been simpler to send *Carly* away? Or maybe just lock her in the closet? What was she doing taking a helicopter to the top of the earth with a playboy ski instructor…?

The helicopter lurched.

Meredith dropped her phone as her head banged into Josh's shoulder. Josh grabbed her and slid his arm around her, righting her. The helicopter lurched again. Meredith held her stomach, afraid for a moment she might be sick.

"Just breathe," Josh said. "Put your head in your lap and breathe."

Normally, Meredith would've been upset that there was a good chance she would be throwing up next to a handsome man, but she was too queasy to think. Josh rubbed her back and said, "We're almost there, Princess. Hold on."

With a sickening drop, the helicopter landed with a thunk. As they bounced to the ground, Meredith was certain it would plunge right off the mountain. Josh held her steady, keeping a firm grip around her shoulders until the helicopter stopped moving.

"Wind is pretty bad," the pilot said from the front. "Sorry it got a little rough there for a while."

Meredith managed to pick her head up to tell him, "No problem."

"Do you want to go back?" Josh asked. "You don't look well."

"No," she said, shaking her head. As appealing as the offer was, she didn't think she could stand another helicopter ride at the moment. Besides, she had come this far. And she was not a quitter, regardless.

"Look at you," Josh said, giving her a good-ole-boy smack on the back. "What a trooper."

He jumped out of the helicopter and held out his hand to help her down. She waved it away. "I'm fine. I can manage."

Josh shrugged and grabbed his backpack.

Almost immediately Meredith regretted not accepting his help. Why did she always have to be so independent? She grabbed hold of the sides of the helicopter and climbed down to find Josh had already collected his skis and had started walking away. "Don't forget your stuff," he called to her.

Meredith turned back toward the helicopter. The skis were tucked in the back, along with her bag. She'd have to get back in the helicopter to pull them out.

She knew the pilot couldn't help her. He needed to stay at the controls in case the aircraft shifted. Suddenly she was overcome by the stress of the moment. She felt like crying. What was wrong with her?

"Meredith," Josh said, now standing beside her. "If you're not feeling strong enough, we really should go back."

"No." She raised her hands in protest. "I'm fine, really. I just need a few minutes."

"You don't need to prove anything."

"I'm not." She glared at him. She was not some weak little girl. She may not be an athlete but she was no wimp. Even if, she thought, that was exactly how she was acting.

Without asking, Josh reached around her and pulled out her equipment. He looped her backpack over her shoulders.

"Thank you," she said.

"Let's go," he said, carrying her skis and boots. He stopped to pick up his own gear and, when they were far enough away, motioned for the helicopter to leave.

Meredith watched the chopper take off. As it disappeared over the mountain, the whirring sound of the motor was replaced by a thick silence.

For a moment, neither she nor Josh spoke.

They were standing on a plateau, near the side of the mountain. They were surrounded by white-capped mountains. "Amazing, isn't it?" Josh asked. "It's as if we're alone in the world."

She glanced away. The thought was not comforting. She picked up her cell phone and popped it open, looking for messages.

"Meredith," he said sternly. "I think you should put on your skis."

"Just a minute."

Calling her office, she spoke to yet another assistant. After discussing some employee issues, Meredith closed the phone then put it in her pack. Just talking to her office made her feel better. It reminded her that she was not the young naive woman who had last attempted Bear Mountain.

Josh was standing in front of her. His crossed arms made it clear he did not appreciate the wait. Too bad, she thought. She had waited for him.

"As soon as we start to descend, you're probably going to lose reception," he said. "It might do you some good to escape from work for a while."

"No," she said. "It won't. I'm in the middle of a deal."

"Then why are you here?"

"What do you mean?"

"Why aren't you at your office, working?"

"I, well…I…" Her voice drifted off. Once again, she found herself tongue-tied. She couldn't very well explain that he himself was threatening her deal.

"Meredith," he said softly. "I'm beginning to think you were just looking for an excuse to be alone with me again."

Meredith raised her head and laughed. It was an artificial, almost tinny sound. "Hardly."

"Really?"

What could she tell him to convince him otherwise? "The man I'm dating is…he's an excellent skier." The lie just flew off her tongue. "We're going away together next week and I'm afraid I may have exaggerated my skills. I was looking to take a crash course before I leave. I've been so busy that I haven't had time to schedule an appointment."

"I see," he said, his eyes gazing at her coldly. "Why didn't you mention your upcoming ski trip yesterday?"

"Would it have made a difference?" *Play it cool,* she reminded herself. "Besides, it's not exactly your business anyway, is it? I'm paying you to teach me how to ski, not to be my confidant." Or paramour, she thought. For once he was with a woman who could resist his charm. *So there.*

He leaned forward, resting his hands on his poles. "So what's the problem?"

"What do you mean…?" He was motioning toward her feet and the fact that she still hadn't put her boots or skis on. Grabbing her equipment, Meredith tugged on her boots and snapped on her skis. Using her poles for leverage, she straightened and moved beside Josh.

"I'm going to go down a piece first," he told her. "I want you to wait until I stop. Then I want you to ski toward me. Okay?"

She nodded and pulled down her goggles.

Josh took off. He was a gifted skier, twisting and turning with grace and ease. Although he made it look easy, she knew quite a bit of strength was required to tame an unplowed course.

When he got a bit down the mountain he stopped and motioned for her to follow the trail he'd carved out.

Her skis almost sank in the soft powder. Meredith swallowed, worried she had bitten off more than she could chew. Bear Mountain was a difficult run. She had once been an experienced skier, but she was rusty now.

There was nothing she could do about it now. The helicopter was gone. There was only one way down the mountain.

"Here's to you, Carly," she said to herself, sending her sister a silent toast as she pushed off.

She started off trying to go slow. But it was as if she had put on a pair of skates. Her skis slicked over Josh's trail and picked up speed. The wind whistled past her ears as she shot downward.

Hey, she thought. This is fun.

"Wait," Josh commanded, suddenly beside her. He jumped in front of her, forcing her to slow down. "You're losing control."

She nodded. She'd heard what he had said, but she didn't agree. In fact, she was impressed with her performance. She wasn't as rusty as she'd thought.

She took off again, sending a slew of snow heading in his direction.

Josh skied in front of her once again and stopped. She crashed into him, sending them both toppling to the ground.

"What the hell are you doing?" he yelled.

"Skiing. I'm better than I thought," she said.

"Are you kidding? You can't control yourself."

"I can, too!"

"Then why did you run into me?" he asked. He shook his head. "This is too dangerous. What if I had been a boulder?"

What was she doing? Josh was right to refer to her as a princess. That's how she was acting, like a spoiled princess. "I'll go slower," she said.

"I'd rather have you snowplow down this damn thing than risk your life breaking speed barriers. Did you forget how dangerous this can be?"

"I didn't forget anything."

"You forgot everything I taught you."

"Not everything." She blushed as their night together once again popped into her head.

He pushed himself up. "When's the last time you were skiing?"

Hmm. The last time. Well, that would be…last year? No, she had made plans to go skiing but had canceled at the last minute when she'd gotten overloaded with work. And the time before that was… Hmm.

Josh was obviously not happy. "This is unbelievable."

"It's been a couple of years at the most. At the most," she repeated.

"You belong on a beginner slope. Not Bear Mountain. This is the most advanced there is. You should know better, Meredith.''

''I can do better, I can. I just got a little excited, that's all.''

He held out his hand to help her up and she took it. As he pulled her to her feet, she said, ''I'm sorry I ran into you.''

He let go of her hand and adjusted his goggles. ''Snap your skis back on. We'll give it another try.''

When Meredith was fully prepared, he warned, ''Go slow.''

She nodded.

''See,'' he said, snowplowing in front of her. ''This is what I want.''

''But—'' Meredith began.

''No buts. My way or no way.''

Meredith acquiesced and they skied for another hour. Meredith did her best to follow Josh's instructions.

She motioned for them to stop. Josh pulled up alongside her. ''What's wrong?'' he asked.

''Just need a little break,'' Meredith said.

''So,'' Josh asked as they took a moment to rest, ''what's your boyfriend's name?''

''Whose name?''

''Your boyfriend. The guy who's taking you on this ski trip.''

Meredith stopped for a moment, startled. ''Oh, him. His name is…Speed.''

''Speed?''

''That's his nickname. His real name is Tom Jenkins,'' she said, referring to a man who worked for her.

''What does he do?''

''He's an accountant and…very successful.''

"Oh, good," he said. "I was concerned you might be dating someone who was unsuccessful."

"I didn't mean it to sound like that," she said. Her leg slid out from under her, causing her to trip over her skis.

Josh reached out and steadied her. He had a strong, ironlike strength. "Of course not," he said.

"I wasn't," she said again, defensive.

"Then why did you mention it?" His hand was still on her arm.

She paused. "I don't know." She felt terrible. Why had she mentioned it? Was she afraid he might think she was dating someone who was unsuccessful? Or maybe he would think the truth, that she was not dating anyone at all.

"Come on," he said, removing his hand. "Let's keep going. It's none of my business, anyway."

They skied like that for hours, stopping every now and then for him to give her instructions. He was, as she remembered, a patient and talented teacher. At one point, when she had trouble understanding what he was saying about the placement of her legs, he actually held her leg and bent it the way he wanted it to move.

But there was nothing romantic or kind about his touch. It was business, pure and simple.

Just when she was thinking that she was safe, that their time together would pass as student and teacher, they stopped for lunch.

She had been on the mountain since her time with Josh, but she had avoided the cabin. As she looked at it now, she couldn't help but remember a time when their relationship had been anything but professional.

If Josh felt anything remotely similar, he wasn't show-ing it. "I thought we'd take a break here," he said.

It was just as she remembered it, a little log building made by hand with timber from fallen trees found on the mountain.

Josh sat in the snow and unsnapped his skis. She fol-lowed suit then, ignoring the lump in her throat, fol-lowed him toward the cabin.

She felt as if she were in a dream, as if she were moving in slow motion. She walked up the steps to the front porch and entered behind Josh. As it had been years before, the double bed was still pushed up against the wall, its sheets crisp and inviting. The battery-powered refrigerator was still in the corner, a wooden table and chairs in front of it. The stone fireplace was packed full of wood and kindling, ready to be lit at the strike of a match.

"There's no heat," he said, as if just remembering her presence. "Don't bother taking off your coat." Josh opened the refrigerator and from behind him she could see it was stocked with boxed lunches, water, wine and beer. Josh handed her a bottle of water. "Make sure you drink all of it," he said. "Even though it's cold, you can still get dehydrated."

She nodded obediently. Josh took out the lunches and set them on the table. It was obvious he still wasn't speaking to her. She wished she had kept her mouth shut. Why did she have to go and ruin things by making that stupid comment about her ridiculous, imaginary boyfriend? It was as if she had been rubbing "Speed's" success in Josh's face. *He's made it and you haven't.* It was as good as said. While the truth of the matter was that she really didn't care what a man did for a living.

It was much more important that he be sweet and kind.
"Josh," she said, "I'm sorry about that comment."

"What comment?"

"About...Speed. Anyway, I really don't care about
success. I was just saying that he wasn't...well, a nerd.
You know, the whole stigma with accountants."

"No, I don't. After all, aren't you an accountant?"

"My point exactly." She smiled. "But technically,
even though my undergraduate degree was in accounting, I was never an accountant." She hesitated a moment
then said, "I'm surprised you remember my major."

"You'd be surprised at what I remember."

She glanced toward the bed and blushed.

"Anyway, regardless of what your degree is in, you're
hardly a nerd."

She glanced up from her cell phone. "Thanks, but I
define nerd."

"No," he said. "Nerds don't look like you."

Her breath quickened at the compliment.

"Any luck?" he asked, nodding toward her phone.

She shook her head. "No. There's no service up
here."

"So does he practice accounting still?"

"Who?" she asked.

"Tom," he said. "Or Speed."

"Does he what?" She really couldn't stand to continue talking about her imaginary boyfriend.

"Are you okay?" he asked, sitting at the table.

"I'm fine," she said, sitting across from him and unwrapping her sandwich. "What were we talking about?"

"Does this guy still practice accounting?"

"No," she said. "Well, sometimes. He's a comptrol-
ler."

"Ah," he said.

After she had eaten a bite of her sandwich, she decided the time had come to ask the question that had tortured her for two days. "The other night you said you had come back to see Carly. Is there something—" She stopped. Once again, she felt like melting as she looked into his eyes. She glanced away. "Something which I might be able to help with?"

"Unfortunately," he said, "it's not looking like it."

She took another bite. "You must have missed her. I mean, you haven't seen her for years."

He looked at her quizzically. "We kept in touch."

"Oh," she said, trying to ignore the pit in her stomach. "She hadn't mentioned it."

"She probably thought you wouldn't approve."

"Why would she think that?"

"I don't know," he said. "Just a guess."

She forced herself to take another nibble of her sandwich.

"So you do approve?" he asked.

"Approve of what?" she said. Where was he going with this?

"I don't know. My friendship with Carly."

It was almost as if he enjoyed teasing her. What did he want her to say? That because of their rendezvous years ago, he was not allowed to be with her sister?

She forced herself to look at him. She felt the need to say something. But what? *I think that Mark is the best thing that's ever happened to her* or *Keep your hands off my little sister.*

Why was he bothering Carly? Why couldn't he let her get married in peace?

If this morning was any indication, and she was right

about the reason for his tardiness, he was still up to his old ways. Sleeping with a woman had never meant much to Josh Adams. How could Carly be tempted by such a womanizer? How, for that matter, could she?

"Do you want to lay down for a while?"

"What?" She felt as if she couldn't breathe. Was he making a pass? Was he asking if she'd be interested in a little casual sex?

Didn't he hear what she said? She had a boyfriend. A perfectly fine and successful imaginary man who she wasn't about to fool around on.

"It's just that you look a little pale," he said. "Maybe you should take a rest while I check out the best trail for our descent."

She felt like laughing. He was not making a pass. Silly her. "No," she said. "I don't need to rest." *I need,* she thought, *to get out of here.* Quick.

"You're ready to hit the slopes again?"

"Of course," she said. The sooner the better.

The cold air smacked her in the face as she stepped outside. But it did not deter her. In fact, the chill was invigorating. It made her feel capable of charging down the mountain. She snapped on her skis and grabbed her poles.

"Wait," he said, as if he had read her mind. He grabbed her arm, stopping her. "Be careful. The temperatures have dropped in the past hour. It's going to be slippery."

She shrugged off his arm. "I'm more than capable of handling myself."

"I would hate to have you hurt yourself. After all," he said, yanking on his gloves. "Let's not forget what happened the last time we were on this mountain."

And with that, she was off.

* * *

Damn, thought Josh. She was even more frustrating than he'd expected.

He thought about the casual way she had glanced around the cottage, as if seeing it for the first time. She had made no mention of their night together. And she was obviously irked by his continued friendship with Carly. Meredith was high and mighty one minute, coy and demure the next.

He found himself anticipating the look on her face when she found out that he was the competitor she was fighting so hard to stave off. If she had been kind, or even polite, he would have confessed. But her behavior made him realize he was correct: Meredith was an uptight, narcissistic woman who was begging to be taught a lesson.

But still, he thought, she could be so self-deprecating. Like the way she had referred to herself as a nerd. Surely she knew otherwise. It was just a ploy. One he had heard before. She was begging for a compliment, looking for proof that he was still interested in her.

Well, she wasn't about to get it. He had no interest in her any longer.

Or did he?

If he had known why she was so anxious to return to Bear Mountain, he never would have agreed to the lesson. But why would her having a boyfriend make any difference? Unless...unless he had come with ulterior motives.

He ran a gloved hand through his hair before yanking his hat back on.

Damn.

He hated to admit it, but more than once he had found himself remembering the way she had felt in his arms, the feel of her creamy-white skin pressed up against him. The way it had felt to be inside her. To know that no one—no one—had had her but him.

But that was years ago, he reminded himself. It would not be the same. His naive virgin had turned into a corporate vixen.

He was snapped out of his reverie as Meredith moved out of his line of sight.

What was she doing? She was going too fast. He had told her to slow down but she'd refused to heed his warning. It was as if her power and prestige gave her a feeling of invincibility. She was a fool, daring the mountain in a game she would not win.

Personal feelings aside, however, he had no intention of watching her jump off a cliff.

He raced after her, determined to stop her by throwing himself in front of her again if need be.

''Meredith,'' he called. But she ignored him. He sped up, trying to overtake her on the pass. He took a jump and landed beside her. Once again, he yelled for her to stop. But he could tell from the look on her face that she was not enjoying her ride. Meredith had lost control.

He motioned for her to drop to the ground. He knew the minute she hit, her skis would release.

She gave a quick nod and attempted to sit. But Meredith didn't go straight down. She panicked and lost her balance. She began a downward spiral.

He threw himself in front of her, breaking her fall.

Meredith crashed into him. Together they formed a living snowball, tumbling down. Finally, Josh rolled to a stop. He lifted his head to see Meredith laying on the ground, motionless. "Meredith!" he yelled, rushing toward her. "Can you hear me?"

Her beautiful eyes blinked open. "Yes."

He dropped his head down as relief flooded through him. This was his fault, all his fault. He never should've brought her up here in the first place. After all, it had been years since he had given a ski lesson. He was the arrogant one, not her. And his arrogance had almost killed her.

"I'm sorry, Josh. I tried to stop, I did…"

"It's okay," he said. He stripped off his gloves. "I'm going to run my hands around you. Tell me if anything hurts."

He slid his hands under her and touched her shoulders. "Fine," she said.

He kept going, working his way down her back. When he reached her rear end, she pushed him away. "I'm fine," she said as she tried to stand. "Ouch!" She plopped back down. "It's my ankle."

He glanced at her ankle. It was the same one she had pretended to hurt all those years before. He looked at her, confused. Was this some sort of game? Was this part of an elaborate plan to seduce him?

Meredith had turned a crimson red, as if she was reading his mind. "It really is hurt," she said quietly.

He saw Meredith wince as he touched her ankle. The pained look in her eyes was very real.

Right away he felt a sense of guilt for even thinking that she had faked it. How could he be so narcissistic?

He sighed. They had no choice but to return to the cabin. He would arrange to have a helicopter drop off a gurney at the only place one could land—the top of the mountain. He would pick up the gurney and come back for her.

"Okay," he said. "Can you walk?"

She shrugged. "With help."

He leaned over and pulled her arm around his shoulder. "When I say three, we're going to try to stand, okay? One...two...three!"

With a great effort, Meredith stood. She accepted his help without reservation. He could tell by her labored breaths that she was in pain. "Are you okay?" he asked.

She nodded. He had to hand it to her. Meredith was tough.

"We're going to head back to the cabin," he told her. "Lean on me as much as you can."

Meredith shifted her weight to lean against him. Her head rested on his shoulder. He inhaled the clean, sweet smell of her hair. "Okay," he said, fighting for concentration. His arm slipped lower to rest on her hip. It was firm and tight. "Let's go."

They started to hike back up the mountain, moving as slowly as possible.

Meredith couldn't believe her bad luck. She'd meant to go slow—she had. But once again she'd found herself speeding down the mountain, heading toward a rather frightening-looking jump. In her younger days, she would've taken it with gusto, but this time she'd known she wasn't up to it.

Obviously, Josh had been thinking the same thing. But when he'd motioned for her to stop, she couldn't do it properly and had found herself tumbling down the mountainside, taking Josh with her.

The next thing she'd known, Josh had been leaning

over her. Just like that, she'd been transported down memory lane. And like a seductive fantasy, his eyes were just inches from hers. The pain in her ankle had been nothing compared to the feel of his hands on her body—even though he'd just been searching for injuries.

She had pushed him away, afraid that she might murmur some intelligible sweet nothings if he continued. And then, to realize she had hurt the same ankle she had pretended to hurt all those years before...

Her mother and sister's well-laid plan was a mess. Here she was, hobbling back to a cabin that she had made love in all those years ago. It was no longer Carly who needed rescuing, but her.

"How are you doing?" Josh asked. He was practically carrying her, but he had not even broken a sweat.

"Fine. What about you?"

"I'm not the one with the hurt ankle."

"No. You're the one with the dead weight."

He smiled. "You're not dead weight."

"I'm not light weight."

"You are," he said. "You're a lightweight."

"Very funny." She continued to hobble along. "What will we do once we get back to the cabin?"

"We'll do the same thing we did before when you hurt your ankle. Remember?"

She stopped breathing. Sure, she remembered. She remembered lying on that bed and making love to him for hours. Remembered wishing that she could spend the rest of her life right there in his arms. Remembered...

"We'll call for help," he said. "I'll meet the helicopter and come back with a gurney."

"Oh," she said with relief.

"Did you have something else in mind?" he asked.

"Of course not," she said tartly. From the corner of her eye, she could see a hint of a smile. "Are you laughing at me?"

He stopped walking. "I would never laugh at you, Meredith."

What seemed like hours later, they reached the cabin. He helped her to the bed and sat her down, before walking over to the radio.

"How long will it take you to climb up the mountain?" she asked him.

He shrugged. "A couple of hours."

She glanced at her watch. "It might be dark by then."

"I hope not."

"Why?"

"If it's dark, they won't land. Too dangerous."

Meredith listened as Josh radioed in to the park rangers. The news was not good. Over the intercom she heard the rangers tell him that no helicopter would be able to rescue them. The wind had picked up. It was too dangerous.

Josh sighed and signed off. After a pause he turned toward her. "So we're stuck here."

"Looks that way," she replied. Just hours ago she had been anxious to get back down the mountain, but now all she could think about was how disappointed Josh looked. It was as if he couldn't imagine anything worse than being stuck here with her. Not that she blamed him. Her behavior had been horrid.

Josh walked over to the table and began to take off his boots.

"I'm sorry," she said. "If I hadn't gone so fast..."

"You're right," he said. "If you had listened, we wouldn't be stuck here right now."

So he *was* angry with her. "It wasn't intentional."

"Accidents never are. But speed usually is."

"I tried to slow down."

"Not hard enough."

She crossed her arms. His belligerence was not helping. "I didn't do this on purpose, you know," she snapped.

"Are you sure?"

She felt as if she couldn't breathe. Was he insinuating that she had faked this sprain...much like she had faked the last one? "What's that supposed to mean?" she heard herself ask.

He shook his head, as if disgusted. "I'm going to get some more wood," he said. "We might as well get comfortable...and make the best of this situation." With that Josh walked out of the cabin, the door banging shut behind him.

She remembered that there was a small woodshed out back. Every fall it would be stocked with enough wood to warm the cabin all winter if need be. It was an unnecessary precaution, since the cabin was never intended as a permanent home. It was simply a place for respite from a sudden storm, a temporary shelter from the cold and often brutal terrain. Many skiers had found themselves trapped here, unable to continue their descent. It was restocked as necessary with enough supplies to last the emergency campers a week.

The mere thought of being alone with Josh made her cringe. She wasn't sure she could manage being alone with him for a night, but a week? What in the world would she talk to him about? She had little in common with this professional playboy. Not to mention her office—what would they do without her?

She took a breath. She was letting her imagination run wild. They would not be stuck here a week. And she could certainly handle a night. After all, she thought, what's the worst that could happen?

"Why don't you get into bed?" Josh said. He was standing in the doorway. His arms were loaded with wood.

"What?" she asked.

"The bed," he repeated, nodding toward the corner. "You should keep your foot elevated."

"Oh," she said. The bed, of course. Keep her foot up. "I'm fine here." She settled back on the couch as she watched him stack the wood. "When were you here last?" she asked.

He put some extra kindling in the fireplace, lit some paper and tossed it in. And then he turned around to face her. "With you."

He paused for a moment, staring into her eyes. It looked as if there was a hint of…anger? Or was it regret?

He turned back toward the fire. "There," he said as the flames leaped up. "We should be warm in no time." He nodded at the refrigerator. "Do you want something to drink?"

She shook her head.

"You should at least take off your boot," he said.

She nodded and bent down. Her foot was throbbing. Suddenly her eyes were filling with tears. What had she done? This entire plan was ridiculous. And now she was stuck on a mountain with someone who obviously couldn't stand up. She blinked away the tears.

"I'm sorry," Josh said, sitting beside her. He motioned toward her sore ankle. "I know that hurts." He unsnapped her boot and gently pulled it off. He removed her sock and ran his fingers over her black-and-blue, swollen foot. "It looks pretty bad."

"I'm fine," she said, pulling her foot away.

He walked to the freezer and took out an ice pack. Then he opened his backpack and pulled out an Ace bandage.

Without saying a word, he knelt in front of her. He wrapped her ankle tenderly and slowly, treating her more like a lover than a difficult client. "We'll replace the ice in a half hour."

"You've obviously had experience with this sort of thing."

He nodded. Then he looked at her and hesitated, as if deciding what to do with her. "You really should lean back and put your foot up." He went to the cupboard and returned with a glass of water and some ibuprofen. "Take this," he said.

She swallowed the pills like a dutiful child and handed him back the glass.

He said, "I'm going to see what I can find for dinner."

She closed her eyes. In the background she could hear him rooting through the cupboards. As much as she didn't think she could sleep, she could feel the effects of the pain and medication taking their toll. It was, she knew, going to be a long night.

Four

Josh was frustrated. He never should have taken Meredith on this crazy adventure. He was not a ski instructor anymore. How could he have thought that he could handle a student on Bear Mountain, especially when that student was as notoriously stubborn as Meredith Cartwright?

He glanced at Meredith. She had been sleeping for more than an hour. The ice pack should be changed, but he didn't want to wake her. He glanced over her sleeping form, admiring her gentle curves. Once again, he found himself impressed by her beauty. Her long brown hair fell down her back. Her tiny nose was complemented by her large, full lips. His eyes glanced downward, gazing on her full breasts and...

He forced himself to turn away. It would do little good to pursue anything with Meredith. She was involved with someone. And, from the way she talked, it was serious.

He stood and walked toward the fire. What difference did it make? Meredith Cartwright was not a candidate for a romance with him. And it had nothing to do with her lack of interest in him or her commitment to another man. She was a business rival, plain and simple. One that he was about to leave in his dust.

He checked his watch. The Durans would have received his offer by now. He thought of the reaction at Cartwright Enterprises when they found out the price they'd thought was set in stone had been sent spiraling upward. It would soon be out of their reach. Durasnow would be his, regardless of Carly's marriage.

He looked at Meredith and tipped his head. "Nothing personal, Princess," he whispered.

Her eyelashes fluttered and she pushed herself up. "Hi," she said with a weak smile. "What are you doing?"

He took a fresh ice pack out of the freezer. "We should change your dressing," he said.

She nodded and scooted up. "My ankle feels much better."

"Good." He knelt in front of her and unwrapped her ankle, noticing her wince as he removed the old bandages.

"Do you still think it's sprained?" she asked.

"I don't think it's broken. It might be a sprain. Or you might have torn a ligament. We'll find out tomorrow."

She nodded. He finished wrapping her up. As he started to walk away, she grabbed his wrist. "Thank you," she said.

For a moment he felt a sting of remorse. Her big brown eyes seemed to sear through him, sizzling through the barrier around his heart. He thought of the offer and the misery awaiting her when she finally managed to get through to her office.

Forget it, he told himself. It was too late for sentiment.

He handed her a stick he had found outside. "If you need to walk," he said.

"Thanks." She pulled herself to her feet, using the stick as a crutch. "Did you find anything for dinner?"

"There's some boxed things in there. Crackers and such."

"I hope I can do better than that." She hobbled to the open cupboards. "Tuna fish. Noodles. Mushroom soup. Tuna casserole," she said.

He smiled. "You know how to make tuna casserole?"

"What's so funny about that?"

"I can't imagine you even eating tuna casserole."

Her smile faded. "You think I'm just a typical rich girl."

"Not typical, no. I think you're a very hard worker."

"I am. And I'm not like some of the other women you might know. I realize I seem that way sometimes, but my life has not been easy."

"I know that, too," he said. "I was sorry to hear about your dad."

"He wasn't my dad. He was my stepfather. And he was a slimeball." She handed him the can. "Would you mind opening this for me?"

"Harsh words for the man who had been a part of your life for a long time." He grabbed the can opener.

She was looking at him. "You think I'm heartless."

"Are you?" he asked, opening the can.

She shrugged. "I don't think so. He and I never got along. I knew about his affairs and it made me sick. And he devastated our company. My mother never should've given him the reins."

"Why did she?"

"My mother loved him." She turned away and ripped open the package of noodles. "It's this thing the women in my family have. It's like they can't help themselves. They always seem to fall in love with the bad boys."

"Bad boys?" he asked, putting the open can on the counter.

"Men who are no good for them."

"Including you?"

She stopped moving. "No," she said finally.

"So," he said, taking a step closer to her, "this boyfriend of yours is a nice guy?"

She shrugged uncomfortably. "I really don't want to talk about him."

"Why not?"

"Because I, well…I just don't."

He nodded. Time to back off. "Okay," he said. He leaned back against the counter. "What about Carly, then? Is this future husband of hers a 'bad boy'?"

"Mark?" Meredith seemed to relax at the mention of her future brother-in-law. She turned around and smiled. "No. He's wonderful. Kind, smart, loyal. You couldn't find a better man."

Her description of her future brother-in-law could not have been warmer. He couldn't help but notice the way her eyes got all dreamy as she described him.

The muscles in his jaw tightened. Was she in love with her future-brother-in-law? "Too bad Carly got to him first."

"Mark?" She looked at him, obviously surprised by the vehemence of his reaction. "I'm not interested in Mark."

Of course she wasn't. She was interested in what he was bringing to the table. Thus the dreamy look. "Just his parents," he said.

"What's that supposed to mean?"

"It means you want a product that, coincidentally or not, is manufactured by the Durans."

"How do you know about that?"

"The newspapers, of course."

"In Europe?"

"I get the U.S. papers off the Internet."

"The Durasnow connection," she said, hesitating, "is a coincidence. Mark's a heart surgeon. Carly met him at a dinner party and fell in love. Only after she was dating him did I make an offer on Durasnow." She looked at him as if sizing him up. "I have to admit I'm surprised by your interest. But then again, you always did care about Carly. I guess it makes sense that you've kept tabs on her."

"Carly's a friend who I haven't spoken to in years, Meredith."

"Okay," she said.

He could tell she didn't believe him. And for some damn reason, he felt the need to convince her. "I'm a fan of the *New York Times*'s business section. You're mentioned quite a bit."

"If you read the *Times,* then you know very well I'm not a fan," she said. "There's been a lot of unflattering press about Cartwright."

"But they've been kind when discussing you. It's

clear the company's travails are not your fault. You inherited them.''

''And we're back on my stepdad.''

''I'm surprised the board let your stepfather stay in power so long.''

''They regret it.'' She sighed. ''I've worked really hard to bring the company back. It hasn't been easy. I have a lot of pressure on me. My business, my family. Everyone is counting on me.''

She handed him another can. ''I know I have this reputation for being hardheaded and cold…''

''Meredith,'' he said, accepting the can. ''You don't have to defend yourself.'' He finished opening it and handed it back to her.

Their fingers touched. Meredith did not pull away. ''I know what you think of me, Josh.''

''What are you talking about?''

''I know what everybody thinks. That I'm a nasty woman who deserves whatever she gets.''

''That's not true,'' he said, knowing he should pull away.

''What do you think of me?'' she asked.

Her lips were full, almost pouty. They were lips begging to be kissed. ''Does it matter?''

''If it didn't, I wouldn't ask.''

His gaze dropped down. Her nipples were hard, her breasts rising and falling with each breath.

He remembered taking off her turtleneck and freeing her plump, perfect breasts. He remembered touching her soft skin, taking her in his mouth. ''I don't know what to think. I don't know you.''

''You used to,'' she said.

"Did I? Socially perhaps. I thought I knew you better than I did."

She shrugged. "It's not as if we were strangers. I mean, we did sleep together."

"So you *do* remember," he stated, his eyes locking on hers.

"Of course," she said. "I lost my virginity that night. It's something that I'll never forget."

The passion in her voice made Josh pause. He moved away, set the can on the counter, then asked, "Why did you want me to bring you here?"

"I told you. My boyfriend is a skier and…"

"Why not just hit the local slopes? Why Bear Mountain?"

She took a step backward, away from him. "I needed an intense lesson."

He stepped in front of her, so close his mouth was almost touching hers. "Do I make you nervous, Meredith?"

"A little." But she did not back away. It was as if he had dared her, and she wanted to prove she could handle whatever he threw her way.

"Why didn't you ever return my calls after that night?"

"I was embarrassed."

"Embarrassed?"

"I was a virgin."

A tendril of hair fell over her forehead. He reached out and slowly, gently, brushed it away from her eyes. "I remember."

She blinked, catching her breath. "I just…well, I know—knew—your reputation. I knew that it meant nothing to you. I didn't want you to think that I was going to hound you or something.''

''But I was the one calling you.''

Meredith shook her head. ''Josh, I know…my limitations. And I'm not stupid. I knew that if we hadn't been trapped here, you never would've slept with me.''

''You're right about that.''

Meredith swallowed and nodded.

''Because I wouldn't have had the nerve to ask you out.''

''What?'' She shook her head. ''You never even noticed me.''

''Why do you think I made love to you?'' He leaned forward, unable to stand the temptation any longer. He had to kiss her, to feel the touch of her lips against his. To take her in his arms…

''You were bored?'' Meredith shrugged and turned away from him. She took the open can and dumped the contents into a bowl.

The spell was broken. Reality came crashing back.

What the hell was he thinking? He had been about to kiss her! It was pointless to discuss the past. Whatever had happened was over. He could no longer afford a dalliance with Meredith Cartwright.

''You never told your sister what happened between us, did you?''

She shook her head.

''Why not?''

''Because it was between us. Something special. I felt like if I told anyone it might take some of that away. It was too personal. What did your friends think when *you* told them?'' she asked.

''I never discussed you with my friends.''

"Why not?"

"Because I never discuss the women I've been with."

"Oh," she said, glancing away as if slighted.

Surely she wasn't jealous about other women? "I'm sorry," he said. "Sorry I brought this up. Let's change the subject."

He watched her stir the mushroom soup. Meredith Cartwright making a tuna casserole. Yet it did not look as ridiculous as it sounded. In fact, Meredith looked just as comfortable in a one-room shack with no heat as she did her ten-thousand-square-foot family mansion. "I admire you, Meredith," he said finally.

She stopped stirring and looked at him as if she was stunned.

"What you've done with the company," he added quickly.

A flash of relief seemed to cross her face before she turned back to the bowl. "You probably have a different woman cooking for you each night," she said.

"What makes you say that?"

"It's who you are. Mr. Ski Instructor. Mr. Seduction."

"A lot of time has passed, Meredith. People change."

"So you're no longer with a different woman each night?"

"I was never that bad," he said.

"You were pretty bad."

He shrugged. "I've always liked women. And I've always liked sex." *Especially,* he wanted to add, *with you.*

She blushed and glanced at the casserole.

He swallowed. Perhaps they didn't need to keep it

professional. Perhaps, if Meredith was willing, they could share some intimate time together.

"But," he said, taking her hand, "I was definitely not the playboy you think I was. I may have dated a lot of women, but I didn't sleep with them—regardless of what you may have heard."

She glanced at him.

He asked, "Do you remember the Black and White Ball?"

"Of course I remember," she said. "You brought Lauren Hughes."

He had long ago forgotten who he had brought to that party. All he remembered about that night was talking to Meredith. "You remember my date?" he asked, surprised.

"I still see her sometimes. She's married now, but every bit as pretty."

"I barely remember her."

She smiled slightly, as if pleased by his admission. "Everyone there had a date except me. So I took myself on a tour of the house. I ended up in the library." She shrugged.

"And that was where I found you," he said. He could remember it as though it were yesterday. They had stayed in the library for hours, talking about the pros and cons of living a life like Thoreau. "I thought we connected that night."

"I wouldn't let myself even think something like that. Besides," she said, "if you thought that, why didn't you ask me out?"

"The next day, when I approached you, you were indifferent. I convinced myself I had misread the signals. It was pretty clear that you were not interested."

"So I went off to college and you forgot about me," she said without any detectable malice or jealousy.

"I wouldn't go that far."

She smiled, as if appreciating the effort but not quite believing the words. "And then I booked you for a private lesson."

He took a step toward her. "I didn't want to embarrass you then, but hell, I'm going to say it now. You didn't need to pretend to sprain your ankle. I would've made a move before the end of our lesson, anyway."

"You knew I faked the sprain?"

"Of course I knew. Just like I know that's a *real* sprain." He pointed to her ankle.

"Why didn't you say something?"

"Because I didn't want to embarrass you."

When she moved to turn away, he pulled her around so that she was facing him. "My point is that you were then, and are now, a beautiful and intelligent woman. How could I *not* be attracted to you?"

Meredith did move away then, limping over to the couch.

"Now I've embarrassed you," he said.

"No."

"I didn't intend to make you uncomfortable."

"It's okay," she said. "I owe you an apology for the way I behaved back then. It was rude of me not to return your calls. I'm sorry."

"I wasn't asking for an apology," he said. "Just an explanation. It doesn't matter. Everything has worked out, right? I mean, you're seeing someone now and you're happy…"

"I guess."

But she didn't look happy. She looked anything but.

Josh wondered about this so-called boyfriend of hers. Perhaps it was not as serious as she'd made it out to be. Or perhaps he was mistreating her. Perhaps she had been referring to her own experiences when she'd spoken of the Cartwright women's disastrous relationships.

He moved toward the couch. "Let's change your bandage again."

"I can do it," she said.

"That's all right," he told her. He held on to Meredith as she sat, then knelt in front of her. He took his time, slowly unwrapping the bandage. It was nice to be close to Meredith, nice to be caring for her. "It's looking a little better." He ran his fingers around the base of her ankle and noticed that Meredith closed her eyes as if she relished the touch. His touch. "How does it feel?" he asked.

"Better."

He got another ice pack and secured it, surprised by the tenderness of his feelings. Surprised, even, by the surge of guilt. He wanted to be open with Meredith. He wanted to tell her the truth about who he was and why he had come back. He could not stand to keep up this ridiculous facade any longer.

"There's something I need to tell you."

Before he could continue, the shortwave radio interrupted them. "Come in, Josh... Josh, do you read?" The voice crackled through the room, shattering the quiet intimacy.

Josh jumped as if someone had just caught them in the act. He ran his fingers through his hair and muttered a quiet, "Damn."

Meredith did not start to breathe until Josh turned

away. What was happening between them? She could've sworn that Josh had been about to kiss her.

"Yeah," Josh replied over the radio mike. "Right here."

"Look, Josh, I've got a guy here who says he needs to talk to Meredith. Tom Jenkins. He says he works for her."

Tom Jenkins…i.e., Speed? Her imaginary boyfriend interrupting the imaginary lovers. Meredith could feel her face burn red with embarrassment.

Josh raised an eyebrow. He turned back toward the mike and said, "Sure. Go ahead and put Speed on. She's right here."

Meredith hobbled to the radio. Josh pulled out the chair and motioned for her to sit. When she was settled, he reached over and pressed the button to communicate. "Hello?" she said.

"Meredith," said the voice on the other end. "This is Tom. Look, we've got a problem. The phantom company has supposedly made another bid."

"When?" Meredith asked. Josh let go of the transmit button and stepped back.

"This morning. They're not fooling around. They've doubled their bid."

"How do you know?" she asked.

"Duran called. Said there was something to be said for relatives but that this company was making things very difficult."

Meredith's heart sank. She knew what that meant. The product was still theirs, but it was going to cost them more.

"Listen, Tom, I want you to sit tight. Don't make a move until I get back."

"When's that going to be?"

"Maybe tonight," she said.

"All right, Meredith," Tom said. "Sounds great. What do I say now? Ten-four?"

"Hey, Josh," the park ranger said as he came back on. "Don't do anything stupid, okay?"

"We're not going anywhere," Josh told him. "We'll contact you in the morning." He disconnected and turned back toward Meredith. "You and your boyfriend sure talk a lot of sweet nothings."

Meredith glanced away. "We were distracted by business. And we knew other people were around. We're not much for public displays of affection."

"Right," he said.

"Josh, I have to get back down the mountain."

"No way."

"I can't stay here," she said. "There is something very important happening at work. They need me."

"You have a hurt ankle."

"I can make it," she said. "I can strap on the ski boot and get down. I can go on one ski, if necessary."

"It's almost dusk. We're not going down a mountain in the dark."

"Why not? You've done it before."

It was true. Josh had been a notorious risk-taker and had been known more than once to traverse a mountain in the dark. "Not for a long time."

She stood trying hard not to wince. She ignored the throbbing pain in her ankle and said, "It feels much better."

"No."

"I'll pay you for your trouble."

"Forget it." His voice was a growl.

"What's it worth? A thousand. More?"

"How high are you willing to go?" He took another step, standing so close she could feel his breath against her cheek.

"I'll do whatever it takes."

He touched her cheek. "Whatever?"

What was he insinuating? Did he want to sleep with her? And what if he did? Would that be so bad? They could have sex and then go their separate ways. Just like they had before. "Okay."

He leaned forward and for a moment she though he was going to kiss her. She closed her eyes, waiting for the kiss. "No deal," he whispered in her ear.

Her eyes snapped open. He was looking at her as if she were a piece of soiled meat.

"You are incredible. You'll stop at nothing to get what you want."

"I don't know what you're talking about," she said quickly. It was a trick. A minefield. And she had limped right into it.

"Really?" He moved closer again. "You would've sold yourself to get back down that mountain, wouldn't you? And for what? A business deal?"

No! she wanted to scream. The only person she would have ever said yes to was him. But he would never believe that. Better to act as if there was a misunderstanding. "I don't know what you're talking about."

"You have to be one of the hardest women I have ever met. God only knows what you're like in the boardroom. Is this how you've made it, Meredith? Do you often offer yourself to make the deal more appealing?"

She slapped him. The sound cracked across the room. "How dare you."

He shook his head, grabbed his coat and stomped out.

Meredith sank back on the couch, humiliated. He was right. She had behaved like a tramp. But it was only because she really did like him…she really did have feelings for him.

Oh, no. She still cared about Josh. All these years, all this time apart, and he still made her want to rip off her clothes and jump into his bed. Every touch, accidental or not, caused her body a flurry of delight. And every time he looked into her eyes and spoke with his heavy, soft drawl, she wanted to kiss him.

She had to put him out of her mind and focus on the problem at hand. She needed to get down the mountain. The sooner the better.

Josh gathered up the branches and headed back toward the cabin. He felt like he was functioning in slow motion, so focused was he on his interaction with Meredith. He had heard about her cunning tactics in the boardroom, but he never thought that she would actually sleep with someone to seal the deal.

The prude and proper girl he had known all those years before would never have agreed to that. Apparently Meredith had lost all sense of self-respect.

So be it. Josh Adams could not be bought.

He wondered what she would think if she knew that he was the reason for her desperation. If her boyfriend had waited a few minutes more, she would've known. But he was glad he had not had the opportunity to tell her who he was. Perhaps the Meredith he had been so touched by was not real…perhaps she had been playing him.

In any case, he should have sympathy for her. She

was about to lose the only thing she really cared about. Her business.

He opened the door to the cabin. It was empty. He looked toward her skis. They were gone.

Merde! he swore. He put out the fire, grabbed his skis and headed back out. He didn't mind if Meredith lost her business. But he didn't want her to lose her life.

Five

Josh shone the flashlight on the snow in front of him. The wind had blown almost all of the tracks away. Fortunately, due to her sore ankle, Meredith had been putting most of her weight on her left leg. The ski had cut deeper on that side, making the trail a little easier to follow.

He skied as fast as he could. What in God's name was she thinking? Was she out of her mind? She couldn't even make it down the slope in daylight, much less in the dark. Yet she was willing to risk her life...and for what?

Despite his anger, he was still impressed. After all, skiing down an unplowed mountain was not easy. Especially with a hurt ankle. Meredith obviously had a high tolerance for pain. But she also possessed a determination unlike any woman he had ever met.

She was one of a kind. And if he had not stormed off, he could've been in bed with her right now, making love.

Instead he had insulted and humiliated her. He had gone too far.

For the second time that day he found himself accepting blame. This was his fault. He was the one who had placed the bid that morning, knowing full well that Meredith would be on the mountain all day, unable to respond. He knew the effect his aggressive bid would have. He was pushing up the price of her product, making it so expensive that she might not be able to afford it.

If anything happened to Meredith Cartwright, he would be responsible.

He glanced ahead. He was coming to a jog on the mountain. It was a jump that Meredith, with her hurt ankle, could not make. Yet her tracks continued, heading straight for it.

He took the jump and landed. He stopped.

He had found Meredith. She was sitting on the ground, her face in her hands.

Whatever anger was left in him evaporated at the sight of her. This was not a person who was capable of taking on the world. This was a vulnerable woman who had been tamed by the mountain.

"Meredith," he said, bending beside her.

She looked at him. "I was foolish, I know."

"Yes," he said. "You're lucky I found you."

She glanced away. "Thank you. I couldn't go any farther by myself. But now that you're here..."

Before she could stand, he took hold of her elbow. The pressure from his grip cut into her as he helped her to her feet. "Let's get one thing straight," he said, in a low, threatening voice. "We're not going back down that mountain until I say so."

She was too stunned to speak.

"Once we get down, you can risk your life on your own time."

She shook her arm away. "I need to get back," she said. "You don't understand. I could lose everything."

"You don't understand," he said, turning his back to her. "I don't care. We're going right back where we came from."

He pulled out a piece of jerky and a bottle of water. He handed her the jerky. "Eat," he said.

She shook her head. "The smell is nauseating."

He opened up her hands and closed them over the jerky. "Either you eat or I'm going to make you eat. You'll never make it if you don't. You're expending too many calories. And you have to drink, as well." He took a swig and handed the bottle to her.

She made a point of wiping off the rim before taking a sip. He raised an eyebrow as if amused. "Worried about germs?" he asked.

She shrugged and handed it back to him. He chuckled before taking another swig. "You are a princess, Meredith."

It took them a good hour to work their way back to the cabin. She made her way as she had earlier, hanging on to his arm. Every now and then she would fall against him and he would steady her, pulling her back up.

He opened the door and helped her to the bed. "It's beyond me, how you managed to get down as far as you did."

"It was painful," she said. "I just tried to block it out."

"You seem to be very good at blocking things out."

He went to the radio and pulled the mike toward him. She could hear him signaling the park rangers.

After a couple of tries, the rangers replied. The news had not changed. She and Josh would be stranded there for the night.

"Wait!" she exclaimed before he signed off.

"What?"

"I wanted to talk to Tom."

"Oh—you mean, Speed? I don't think he was still hanging out with the rangers."

"Obviously," she said testily, hobbling over to the table. "But maybe they could give him a message from me."

As she plopped into the chair, he signaled the rangers once more.

"Go ahead," he said, pointing the microphone toward her. She relayed the message that she had decided that Cartwright Enterprises would counter the phantom company's bid. She was willing to forward half the money up front. When she finished, she stopped for a moment, resting her head against the mike.

It was an important call. She knew her office would be sent into a frenzy, trying to sell whatever assets were liquid. It was a move that could send Cartwright into bankruptcy. But she'd had no choice. She needed Dura-snow, and for all she knew, the other company was about to steal it right out from under her.

"Hey," he said, his hand on her neck. "Are you okay?"

She looked up at him, tears behind her eyes. Suddenly

everything seemed in vain. She had made a terrible mistake coming here with Josh and she was about to pay the price. "Sure. I just…well, I just took a big gamble. That's all."

"You're selling off assets?" he asked softly.

She nodded. "I don't have any choice. The product that…that I want. It could turn around my company."

"But surely there'll be other products."

She shook her head. "No. You don't understand. We don't have the money to go after the really promising ones. I thought that we might have an in with this one because…" Her voice trailed off.

"Because of Carly?"

Josh knew the answer. He wanted to hear her say it. To admit it. But she obviously couldn't.

"No," she said stonily. "Not just because of Carly."

Once again she had shut him out. Just when she'd appeared ready to confide. He shouldn't be surprised. Why *would* she confide in him?

"Although it obviously helps having a family connection," he said.

She stood and crossed her arms in front of her. "I don't think it's shameful to use family connections. After all, our company is not…well, it's not doing very well."

"There's a difference between family connections and familial servitude," Josh said.

She glanced at him. "I know you think I'm just a selfish brat, but I've always worked hard. I've given everything I have to redeeming our family name and gaining back the trust of our investors, but it doesn't look like it's going to work.

She paused for a moment. She looked, once again, as

if she might cry. "Regardless of what you think, I love my sister. I would never encourage her to do something she didn't want to do. Never."

And for once, he believed her.

"Sit down on the bed," he commanded. "I'll get you something to eat."

He turned on the oven and put in the casserole she had made earlier. He thought again about what had driven Meredith to take such drastic actions in the first place. His offer. And another was on the way.

He had directed his assistant to up the offer at five. It was nearly four o'clock as it was. He knew that if Meredith found out, she might just risk her life once again. He couldn't allow that to happen.

He had to reach his office before they made another offer. He needed to tell them to hold off temporarily, at least until he and Meredith made it back down. He glanced toward the bathroom. "Do you want me to run the water for a bath?"

She shook her head. She looked at him and smiled, appreciative of his offer. "Thank you, but that's not necessary. Although, I wouldn't mind a shower."

"Go ahead," he said. He held out his hand to help Meredith up. She accepted it.

She held his hand and said, "By the way, I owe you an apology."

"For?"

"For earlier. It was one thing to risk my own life but I should've known that you would come after me. I never should have put you in that danger. It was careless and selfish. I'm sorry."

"You've already apologized. Anyway, that's what

you're paying me for, right? To make sure you get down the mountain in one piece."

"I don't think risking your life was part of the deal."

"True," he said. "Maybe I should charge a little extra for that."

She smiled. "I'm grateful to you, Josh."

She sighed deeply. The fading sun lit the window behind her, surrounding her in a warm, hazy glow. He was tempted to kiss her. But he couldn't. He had to cancel his bid while there was still time.

He glanced at his watch. He needed to get the show on the road. "There you go," he said, motioning toward the bathroom. "Towels are in there. Call me if you need help."

"I think I can handle it," Meredith said, hobbling in and closing the door behind her.

Josh signaled the park ranger once again and asked him to forward a message to his assistant.

Josh's message was simple: do nothing until he got back.

When he was done, Josh pushed the microphone away. He knew he was taking a chance. After all, he wanted this product. But he didn't want Meredith to risk her life again. They could deal with the situation when they got down the mountain.

Moving away from the radio, Josh began to light candles. He was warming his hands against the roaring blaze when the bathroom door finally creaked open. He looked up to see Meredith standing with a towel wrapped around her.

"Excuse me," she asked. "Could you hand me my pack? I think I've got some clean leggings and a sweatshirt in there."

He stood still for a moment, forgetting everything but how Meredith looked in a towel.

"It's right there," she said, pointing to the sofa.

He handed it to her. As she reached for it, one edge of the towel fell, but she shut the door before he could see anything else.

He swallowed.

Damn.

He could see her body once again—her lean, flat belly, her full, heavy breasts. Her long, sleek legs.

He reprimanded himself for having such thoughts. He couldn't afford to be sentimental. It was already affecting the way he conducted his business. Why else had he told his people to back off?

Because he cared about her.

More than he might want to admit. But so what? He was a man, wasn't he? And Meredith was an attractive woman.

He busied himself dishing out the plates of tuna casserole and setting them on the table until Meredith came back out. She had dressed in her tight-fitting, silk leggings. The sight was more enticing than if she had come out wearing a negligee.

"Thank you," she said, nodding. "Did I hear you talking to someone?"

He stopped. She had heard him? "I called to find out the weather report for tomorrow."

"And?"

"Some snow. But the wind should stop."

"Good," she said. "So they can come and get us."

"Unless you decide to go for an evening stroll down the mountain again."

She raised her hand. "I promise. I learned my lesson." She smiled once again.

Damn, she was beautiful. He forced himself to look away. He nodded toward the table. "We're ready."

"How nice," she said, looking at the settings. "The fire, the candles. Very ro—" She stopped.

He knew what she had been about to say. Very romantic. He cleared his throat and said, "The setting isn' exactly fancy..."

"I don't care about that," she said. "Most of my meals are takeout."

"This boyfriend of yours doesn't take you out to dinner?"

She looked away. "I usually take my meals at my desk. Unless, of course, I have a meeting or a dinner appointment."

"Doesn't sound like much fun."

She looked at him. "It's not."

He nodded. Wasn't his life the same? Didn't he spend most meals alone at his desk?

She said, "I can't believe I've been gone so long. My mom and Carly are probably very worried."

"They know where you are. I'm sure they'd rather have us take our time and be safe."

"I suppose," she said.

"Start," he said, motioning toward the food.

They settled in at the table. The fire was blazing, casting shadows across the room as they ate. She took a bite and said, "It probably could've used some Worcestershire sauce."

"It's great," he said, swallowing. "So, what does your mother think of this guy Carly's marrying?"

She glanced at him.

He immediately realized his mistake. "I'm not badgering. Honest. Just making conversation."

"Mom loves him," she said, defensive despite his protestation. "He's a really great guy. Totally unlike some of the other men Carly dated."

"I just knew the ones from years ago. I have to say I wasn't impressed much then, either."

She sighed. "Yes, well, that's typical of us."

"That's right. You girls like the bad boys."

"We call it the Cartwright curse. My grandmother married a man that could never stay faithful..."

"Your grandfather?"

"Right. And my dad. I'm sure you heard how he died."

Yes. He had heard the stories of how the man had died in his mistress's bed.

She continued, not waiting for an answer. "And my stepdad...well, I've already spoken about him."

"So your mom and grandmother had lousy taste in men. That's hardly a curse."

"My mother sure thought she was cursed."

"Yet she never divorced either of her husbands?"

"She loved them. You see, *that's* the curse."

"It must have been hard for you. Watching your mother, who seems to be such a strong, capable woman, allowing herself to be treated so poorly."

"Let's just say it's made me more cautious."

"How so?"

She shrugged. "I know that love is something you can't control. If you fall for the wrong person, you're doomed."

"You make it sound as if people have no control over whom they choose to love."

She glanced at him. "Do they?"

"I like to think so."

"I disagree. I think love is just one of those quirks of fate. I think it has more to do with that mysterious thing we call chemistry than anything else."

He was intrigued. She sounded more like a hurt, innocent girl than a woman who had mastered the art of seduction.

"What about Tom?" he asked.

A shadow passed over her face as she looked away. "What about him?"

"Is he part of this curse?"

She paused a moment. She said, "No. He's definitely not part of the curse." She glanced back at him. "What about you? Are you cursed in love?" she asked.

He shrugged. "I don't think I'm cursed. I'm just... well, not blessed with someone special."

"You think that finding someone special, that being in a monogamous relationship, would make you blessed?"

"Yes," he said. "I do. Does that surprise you?"

"A little. I mean, you do—at least, you did—have quite the reputation."

"Am I one of those bad boys you're worried about?"

She gave a small, slight laugh. Pushing back her chair, she stood and lifted her plate to clear it. "No."

He grabbed her wrist, stopping her. "Then why are we here? Why did you ask me to take you skiing?"

"I told you I wanted a crash course..."

"Bull. There are plenty of instructors you could have hired. You haven't seen me in ten years. So answer me. Why, after all this time, did you ask me?"

She broke away and set her plate on the counter. "I don't know. Why did you agree to come?"

He followed her, setting his plate beside hers. "I was curious."

"Curious?"

"Why does Meredith Cartwright want to be alone with me?"

"I told you. I'm going skiing with my boyfriend."

He traced his finger along her slender hand and touched her delicate fingers. "I have a confession to make, Meredith," he said, continuing to caress her fingers. "I like you."

"You don't have to say that."

"It's true, whether you believe it or not. I mean, I'm here, aren't I?"

He kissed the side of her cheek. When she turned her head toward him, welcoming his touch, he held her chin and kissed her softly, delicately. He ran the tip of his tongue around the inside of her mouth, tentatively exploring.

What was going on? Meredith felt as if her world was exploding. She knew she should stop but she couldn't. His hand slipped inside her shirt, searching for her nipple. He found it and folded it in between his fingers, tugging on it gently. She could feel the warmth shoot down into her legs.

"Meredith," he said in his husky, sexy drawl. She knew what was happening was wrong, but she couldn't help herself. Her body had overruled her mind. She had deprived it too long.

"Meredith," he said, pulling away. "What's wrong? Where did you go?"

"Nothing is wrong," she said.

"Is it Tom?"

Suddenly, Meredith saw Tom in her mind. In his early sixties, bald, about thirty pounds overweight.... She wished she had never made up that ridiculous story. For all Josh knew, she had a hottie waiting for her back in Aspen.

She didn't want him to think that she was the kind of woman who could sleep around. She wanted him to realize exactly who she was. "Tom's not really my boyfriend."

"Oh?"

"No," she said. "I just, well…"

"It's okay, Meredith," he said, kissing her neck. "You don't have to explain.

"There's something you should know," she said. "And it may make you change your mind about me."

"What?"

"I…well…I haven't slept with anyone since—well, since…since the last time we were here."

His eyes narrowed.

There. She had done it. He saw her now as she saw herself. A freak. A sexual oddball. The kind of woman who turned guys off…

Josh pulled her to him, kissing her hard…hot…intensely. When they came up for air, he asked, "Why not?"

"Well," she said, barely able to speak, her heart was pounding so hard. "I just…well, I've been busy."

He cradled her face in his hands. "Too busy to make love?"

"I didn't have time to get emotionally involved with

anyone. I didn't see how I could separate my business and private lives.''

''But you can with me?''

''I'm willing to try,'' she said.

His eyes scanned her face as if deciding what to do with her.

''I shouldn't have told you,'' she said, turning to move away, but he quickly pulled her back into his arms.

The look in his eyes made her blood quicken. It was wild and dangerous. Meredith had the feeling they had passed the point of no return.

''Meredith,'' he said hoarsely, touching her hair, caressing her with his rough fingers. She expected him to crush her with passion, but when he kissed her, it was soft and gentle. He took his time, welcoming her mouth like a long lost friend.

She reached up and touched his face. This was not a dream, she thought. It was real. Real.

His tongue parted her lips and entered her mouth, probing and teasing. Meredith could feel her knees grow weak as he continued, tasting and exploring. This was not the kiss of an amateur. This was the powerful kiss of a man who knew how to pleasure a woman.

She arched her back as she reached her hands around his neck. With his lips still on hers, he swept her off her feet and carried her to the bed. He laid her down, still kissing her.

She reached for him, pulling him on top of her. His hands swept over her, caressing her through the soft material of her sweatshirt. He yanked her shirt up and freed her breasts from her bra. His lips found her nipples, taking turns with each, softly biting and sucking until she felt ready to scream with pleasure.

As his hands moved to remove her leggings, he paused to murmur, "You are so beautiful. So beautiful."

She was naked but she did not feel the least bit modest. She wanted him to look at her. She wanted to feel his eyes on her, to feel him touching her. She needed him. Taking his hand, she placed it on her lower belly.

She didn't need to say a word—he knew exactly what to do.

Josh gave her a wicked smile, one that said he appreciated her eagerness. His hand slipped between her parted legs, caressing and teasing as he worked his way toward her most sensitive part.

As he gazed into her eyes, studying them for signs of pleasure, he touched her with his index finger. He rubbed her back and forth, causing a stream of warmth to surge through her body. She sighed, closed her eyes and arched her back as she moved herself against him.

He bent over her, teasing her with his tongue, laving her gently and slowly, just as he had kissed her. His tongue moved back and forth, softly at first, then with increasing pressure.

The feel of his breath against her combined with the sensation of his tongue scorched though her. She couldn't think of anything but her impending release.

"I want you, Josh," she heard herself moan as she reached for him, fumbling with his belt.

"Not yet," he said, touching her hands. He placed each of them above her head, to wrap around the bedposts.

She felt totally exposed, her arms and legs in invisible bonds. She lay spread-eagled, watching him take off his shirt. He was moving slowly and calmly, as if he was enjoying the knowledge that she was waiting for him.

"Don't move until I tell you," he said, smiling wickedly once again.

He towered over her, his powerful, well-muscled body glimmering in the candlelight. "I can't take my eyes off you," he breathed, admiring her from the edge of the bed before moving to sit beside her.

Meredith fought her instincts, keeping her hands wrapped tightly around the post as he had instructed. She felt dangerously vulnerable, but the vulnerability only heightened the eroticism.

It was clear he was not about to rush their lovemaking. Josh was a man who was as comfortable in the bedroom as he was on the ski slope.

He cradled her face in his hands and kissed her. Once again, his tongue slipped inside her mouth. At one point she instinctively let go of one of the bedposts to touch him, but his hand was on hers immediately, placing it back on the post.

He ran his fingers down her body, looking and touching, exploring her like a delicate statue. He took her nipples in his mouth as he reached between her legs.

"Please," she begged. "Now."

"Look at me," he said, as he moved over her.

As her eyes met his, he entered her.

She lifted her hips toward him, taking him deeper. She continued to stare into his eyes as he moved inside her. Unlike the first time they had made love, she felt no pain. It was as if he were a perfect fit.

He moved slowly, and she held to the bedpost tightly as the momentum built. She felt wild and uninhibited. Willing to do anything for release.

A cold breeze blew through the cabin. The candles flickered, causing the light to dance across the room.

Their shadows reflected on the wall: together they had become one.

The feeling continued to build as he rubbed against her. She held so tightly to the bed that her fingers were white from the pressure. Suddenly...suddenly...

The dam burst free, causing years of denied pleasure to rock through her. They clung to each other as the liquid warmth fused them together.

She opened her eyes. The danger in his was gone, replaced by kindness. He took her hands from the bedpost, kissing her fingers and holding them before lying beside her.

Neither spoke. They just lay there, side by side. Every now and then Josh would run his hand over the side of her arm or across her forehead. And every now and then she would glance over at him, checking to make sure he was still here. That it wasn't a dream.

After a while he pushed himself up on one arm, facing her and asked, "Are you all right?"

The sound of his voice was enough to bring Meredith spiraling back to earth. Suddenly she remembered her reason for being here in the first place. *Carly.*

"Yes," she said.

What if Carly really did care about him? How would she explain this to her sister?

"Close your eyes," he said. He stretched out, the body of a panther. "Try not to think."

Meredith shut her eyes. When sleep came, she welcomed it.

Josh lay awake, staring at the woman asleep beside him. Loose tendrils of her luxurious, thick hair framed her ravishing face, made even more radiant by the soft blush of sex. She sighed slightly and the mere sound was enough to make his body ache once again for her touch.

What had he done?

He was in the midst of a complicated business deal, and he had slept with the opposing bidder. What made matters worse was that she had no idea who he was. He had deceived her.

He needed to tell Meredith who he was. He owed her that much.

Damn. How had he lost control like that? Was it hearing that he had been her only lover? Had his ego found the opportunity too rare to turn down?

The truth of the matter was, he had been attracted to Meredith from the moment he'd seen her in the library at that party. He had hoped that time would have lessened his reaction to her, taken some of the intensity out of his attraction. But it hadn't.

The attraction had only gotten worse.

He could've handled himself had she stayed distant. If she had continued her feisty I-don't-need-anyone-or-anything attitude. But when she'd almost cried after giving instructions to sell her company's assets…

She was a woman who was tough and tender at the same time. She had opened up to him, trusted him enough to let him see her vulnerable and in pain. And he had encouraged it. In spite of himself, he wanted her to trust him. To care about him.

Well, he was a fool. Because once Meredith learned who he was, she would want nothing more than to get away from him.

And it was unfortunate. Because he was just beginning to figure her out.

Meredith was terrified of love, terrified of losing control. So she had attempted to control her first sexual experience as much as possible. It stood to reason that if she could control the environment, she might be able to control her feelings.

She had lost her virginity with him not because of some deep attraction but because he'd been safe. Everyone in Aspen knew he was not the type of man to form a close relationship.

Why hadn't she slept with anyone else since? Plenty of men were interested in sex and sex alone. Had she waited for him? Why?

He ran his fingers through his hair. There was another possibility, one that he didn't relish. For all he knew, she was feeding him a pack of lies. She might know exactly who he was. Perhaps she was playing him, feeding his vain ego, trying to break down his barriers. Perhaps this was nothing more than a complicated boardroom strategy.

Somehow, he doubted that. *No.* He had seen the real Meredith, he was sure of it. She was smart, loyal and kind. She did not deserve to be lied to, especially by a man with whom she had just made love.

He would have to tell Meredith the truth. He was the owner of Europrize.

And he was her enemy.

Six

Meredith opened her eyes. The room was dark with the exception of the blazing fire. She was filled with an overwhelming sense of contentment. Making love with Josh had been everything she could have hoped for. It had been worth the wait.

She turned around and reached out. But she was alone. "Josh?" she whispered. There was no answer.

She gathered the quilt around her and hobbled to the bathroom. The door was open. "Josh?" she said to the empty room.

Where could he have gone?

She opened the front door to find him sitting on the step. "Hey," Josh said, without turning around.

"What are you doing?"

"Thinking." He glanced back at her and grinned. "I didn't follow my own advice."

"Do you want company?" she asked, stepping into the dark, cold outdoors. She needed to be near him. To be touching him.

"No," he said, standing. "It's cold. I'll come back in."

It may have been cold but the view was spectacular. A hush had descended on the snow-covered world. The half moon and thousands of tiny stars twinkled in a solid black sky.

"Stay." She stepped back inside and grabbed her coat off the hook, holding the quilt around her with one hand. "The fresh air feels nice," she said, walking back outside.

Josh took her coat and looped it across her shoulders. Taking her hand, he helped her to lower herself to sit next to him on the step. Pulling her in close, he wrapped his arms around her. "I thought you might have left," she said, half joking.

"Without you?" he said. "I wouldn't do that."

She glanced into his deep gray eyes and felt a pain in her heart. She had expected this reaction—knew what he was thinking. Time to move on. She had opened up and told him more than she should have and now he was concerned that a woman who had waited ten years for sex could certainly not take this situation lightly. "Don't worry about me," she said. "I don't have any expectations."

He hesitated. "Meredith, that's not it."

She took his hand. "What's wrong then?"

He pulled her hands to his lips and sighed. "I haven't been honest with you. And I'm afraid you might have just done something that you're going to regret."

"There's nothing you could say that would upset me."

He touched her chin and pulled her face toward him. "I know the name of the company who's bidding against Durasnow."

"How do you know that?"

"Because I own it."

Pulling back she paused for a moment, smiling. So he had a sense of humor, too. "You're joking."

He stiffened slightly. "I'm the owner of Europrize, Meredith. I'm the other bidder for Durasnow."

"No," she said finally. "You're a ski instructor."

"I haven't taught skiing for years."

"But Switzerland…"

"It's where I live. Where my company is based."

She couldn't think. It wasn't true. It couldn't be. How could she not have known? How could Carly not have known?

"I left Aspen to go to school in London. I found I had a knack for technology. I started creating video games and sold them. Eventually I started my own company."

Meredith couldn't speak. This was not possible. It wasn't.

He continued. "A couple of years ago I started branching out into other things. I bought into a ski resort in Switzerland. I refurbished it, turned the business around. It was successful. One thing led to another. Soon I owned several."

"I don't understand," she said. "Why didn't you tell me who you were when I asked you to take me skiing?"

"I should have, I know. But I was curious."

"Curious?" she said.

''I thought that perhaps you did know who I was.''

''If I did, why would I ask you to take me to the top of Bear Mountain?''

''That's what I wanted to find out.''

Meredith pushed herself to stand. She felt as if she had turned to stone. She had given her body to the man who was trying to destroy her.

''I'm sorry,'' she heard him say.

He was the one who had upped the price on Durasnow. He'd known full well that she would not be around to counter his bid. He had taken advantage of the situation. And she had fallen right into his hands.

''You wanted me out of the way, didn't you? You knew with me here, I'd be unable to respond to any bids. That's why you weren't anxious to get down the mountain.''

''That's not true,'' he said, rising. ''I came back to the States to negotiate with you. I had hoped Carly might broker a deal between us.''

''Carly? Why not approach me directly?''

''Because I didn't think you'd negotiate with me.''

''So, because you didn't talk to Carly, you decided to try to steal Durasnow out from underneath me.''

''I know Wayne Duran. I grew up watching men like him. He's looking for the best deal, plain and simple. And if he thinks he can get more money elsewhere, he'll take it. Regardless of family connections.''

''I'm not a naive schoolgirl,'' she said.

''Look,'' he said. ''When you asked me here, I was flattered. Part of me thought—no, part of me *hoped* that you wanted to be alone with me again.''

''Not anymore,'' she said.

He glanced away. ''I'm sorry.''

"Not half as sorry as I am."

How could she have been so stupid? He was clearly interested in winning Durasnow whatever way necessary.

"Talk to me," he said, grabbing her arm as she started back into the cabin.

She shook off his touch. "What's to say? I'm impressed."

"What does that mean?" he asked, following her inside.

She ignored him as she hobbled over to the bed, grabbed her clothes and went into the bathroom, slamming the door behind her.

Meredith yanked on her clothes as fast as she could. "I underestimated you. I thought you were a decent guy. A ski instructor. It turns out you're a big corporate jerk."

"Look," he said. "Tonight was not a lie. I have feelings for you…"

She slammed open the door and emerged fully dressed. "Don't."

"Don't what?"

"Don't try to romance your way out of this. You plotted against me."

"No," he said. "My interest in Durasnow had nothing to do with you personally."

"Since when do ski resorts go after products? Since when do technology companies—"

"Since now. My company, Europrize, has a variety of interests, the resorts being just one of them. This product will revolutionize the skiing industry. Which is exactly why *you* want it."

She looked at him a long while before she said, "You should know, I *always* win."

"And *I* never lose."

"There's always a first time."

"Yes," he said. "I'm well aware of that."

The wild, sexy look in his eyes told her he was thinking about their lovemaking. Why had she ever told him he was the only man with whom she had been intimate?

"You think your ace in the hole is Carly." He shook his head. "You're wrong. The Durans are playing you, trying to get you to make a counteroffer so they get an even higher price for their product. They have no loyalties to family connections. I'm going to end up with Durasnow and your sister is going to end up in an unhappy marriage."

"That's not true. Carly loves Mark."

"Then why isn't she happy?"

Meredith glanced away. "What would you know about my sister's happiness?"

"I saw her at your party. Drinking too much, flirting…"

"That's just how she is. It doesn't mean she doesn't want to marry Mark."

"Are you sure?" he asked. "Believe it or not, I didn't come back to hurt you."

"I believe that," she said. "You need to care about someone to want to hurt them. I don't think you cared about me one way or another."

"You're wrong. Last night would not have happened if I didn't care."

She flopped onto the bed. This was terrible. Worse than terrible.

"Meredith," he said. "I came back to offer you a deal. It's still on the table. Let's combine forces and go after Durasnow together."

"No way."

"One whiff of bad news about your company and your stock price is going to fall. The Durans will have no choice but to sell to me."

Meredith stood. "Are you threatening me?" She knew what he was implying. Stock prices were rising because of the presumed deal with Durasnow. If word got out that the Durans were thinking about selling to Europrize instead, the value of Cartwright stock would fall.

"I'm trying to reason with you." He moved toward her and touched her shoulder. "Think about it, Meredith. We could be partners."

"There's nothing to think about." She pushed his hand away. "We're not partners and we never will be."

Meredith was thankful when morning finally arrived. She'd barely slept having lain on top of the bed, fully dressed.

She wondered how in the world she would explain herself to her family, not to mention the board. What would they say when they found out she'd been on a skiing trip with the competitive bidder for Durasnow?

She had no one to blame but herself. She had allowed her emotions to get the best of her and she was about to pay a steep price.

Josh, who had sat at the table until daybreak, was speaking to the rangers over the shortwave radio.

When he was finished, he turned to face her. "They're coming," he said solemnly. "They're going to try to pick us up on the north side of the mountain in two hours. And it's about a two-hour walk in the best of conditions." He hesitated. "I had hoped I could go and bring back the gurney for you, but they seem confident that there wouldn't be enough time. The weather situation is too tricky.''

"So I either have to walk up the mountain myself, or we're stuck here for another night," she said, summing up the situation.

He nodded. "At least."

Meredith tired to ignore the dull, throbbing ache of her ankle. *Mind over matter. Mind over matter.*

"Do you think you can make it?"

She nodded.

"What about your ankle?"

"It's much better this morning," she lied.

"Let me see," he offered, taking a step toward her.

She shook her head. "No. It's fine. Really. I'm ready to go."

A thick and heavy silence descended as they closed up the cabin and packed their bags. Meredith felt as if she was moving in slow motion. She was certain if she pinched herself she might just wake up in her own bed in her own apartment.

She waited until the last possible minute to put on her boots. Even though they were much lighter than her heavy ski boots, her swollen ankle still had to be jammed into one. She managed to pull it on, inhaling sharply as the pain tore through her.

She stood to find Josh watching her carefully. But if he was waiting for her to confess her pain, it was for naught. She would do whatever it took to get off this mountain. To get away from him.

She took a step. Ouch! The pain ran up her leg.

Mind over matter, she reminded herself. *Mind over matter.* Meredith shrugged on her coat as she looped the pack over her shoulders. She headed out the door, not bothering to turn around. She never wanted to see the cabin again.

Meredith stepped off the porch and stumbled. Josh caught her just before she hit the ground.

She winced again, clutching Josh out of instinct.

"It's worse," he said, looking at her pain-filled eyes.

"It's fine," she said through gritted teeth.

"We can't go," he said. "I'll call them and explain…"

"No!"

He turned, as if startled by the strength in her voice. "Please," she said. "I have to get home."

He glanced around him, as if considering his options. "Okay. Leave everything here. I'll send someone back for it. Let's just worry about getting you up the mountain." He helped her off with her pack and took it back inside. When he came out, he took hold of her arm and pulled it around his neck. He pulled her against him, practically lifting her off the ground. Then they began their trek back up the mountain.

It was damp and cold. The only sound was the bitter wind and the crunching of snow beneath their feet. Meredith tried her best not to notice how good it felt to lean up against Josh. How nice it felt to have him pull her in close. She kept telling herself that she was not attracted to him any longer. How could she desire someone who had lied to her?

"Meredith," he said finally, "I know I should've told you who I was."

She was silent.

"I'm sorry."

"I want Durasnow," she said.

"I know."

She stopped. "And I'm going to get it."

"We'll see about that."

She began walking again. She slipped and he tightened his grip, righting her. "Easy there, Princess."

"Why did you sleep with me?" she asked.

He glanced down at her. "Why do you think?"

"You were playing me."

"Last night had nothing to do with business, okay? That was about the two of us. You and me. I did what I felt. That's all."

"It's never happening again."

"Whatever you want."

"It's what I want."

"Keep moving," he said.

They went a little farther. Each agonizing step only seemed to add to her anger. "So how long have you been interested in Durasnow?" she asked.

"Ever since I read about the potential for this product years ago."

"The article in the *New York Times*," she said. "I remember."

"What about you?" he asked. "Did you know about Durasnow before you pushed Mark Duran on your sister?"

"I didn't push him on Carly. I already explained that. She had been seeing him months before I even found out about it. She doesn't share everything with me, you know."

"Whatever you say, Princess."

She threw him a wary, suspicious glance. "Carly doesn't know who you are, does she?"

"She knows I'm no longer a ski instructor, but not

my connection to the Durans. They seem to be keeping my identity under wraps. But it was not my intention to keep my identity a secret. When you asked me to take you skiing...well..."

"You knew I had no idea who you were."

"I wasn't sure. For all I knew it could've been some strategy. And I must say, I still don't understand why you would leave your business at a time like this."

Meredith glanced away. It was time to tell him the truth. "I asked you to take me skiing to distract you."

"To distract me? But...you just said you didn't know who I was."

She stopped walking. She had gone this far. Now she needed to finish it. What did it matter anyway? She would never be with Josh. Not now or ever. "You were a..." She hesitated, looking for the right word. "A flirtation that needed to be dealt with."

Josh stepped back, surprised. For a second, he couldn't speak.

She said, "I wanted to keep you away from Carly until Mark returned."

"So there was no impending ski trip," he said, as if stating a fact. How could he be surprised? After all, hadn't he suspected an ulterior motive? "No boyfriend. No need for an emergency lesson."

She hesitated and shook her head.

He could feel his anger grow. "And you slept with me to distract me...or to just quench my thirst, so I wouldn't go hungering after your sister," he said, towering over her. "That was quite a sacrifice on your part."

"I didn't intend for it to go this far."

"You made a mistake, Meredith," he said. "Because I get what I want. And if I had wanted your sister, no one would've been able to distract me."

She bit her lower lip.

"I told you why I wanted to talk to Carly. That was the truth. I wanted Carly to help me get through to you. To help convince you to combine forces."

"Well it doesn't make sense. Why talk to her when you should've been dealing with me directly?"

"Because I didn't think you would negotiate."

"Well, you were right."

He couldn't think about this now. He had to focus on getting them out of here. Luckily, he spotted the helicopter heading their way.

He waved his arms, attracting the pilot's attention. The pilot motioned to a flat area about one hundred feet away. There was just one problem. They had to wade though a snowdrift to get there.

"The snow is too deep," she said.

He glanced at her and then back again. She was right. With her sore ankle, she'd never make it. "Sorry, Princess," he said. "Looks like you're staying."

She put her hand on her hip.

"I'll let you know how everything turns out with Durasnow."

"Very funny," she yelled above the noise of the helicopter. "You'd like nothing better, I'm sure. Leave me stuck on the mountain and…"

Before she could finish, he picked her up. "I'm listening," he said, holding her in his arms. Her eyes widened in surprise. But he didn't have time to play any longer. The helicopter was waiting. He slung her over his shoulder like a sack of potatoes.

"What are you doing?" she yelled.

"Getting you home." He stomped through the deep snow. The helicopter landed, stirring up a small blizzard. Still carrying her on his shoulder, he hit the flat area and moved to the side of the helicopter. Opening the door, he unceremoniously dumped her inside. Then he ran around and jumped in beside her.

She held her head high, twisting away from him as she crossed her arms. They managed to make it all the way back with neither speaking a word.

Seven

"The plan was a disaster," Meredith said as she finished telling Carly about discovering Josh's true identity. The two sisters were sitting in the living room, drinking tea after Meredith had returned from her disastrous trip up the mountain and a stop at the hospital for some X rays and a tight bandage for her sprained ankle.

"How can you say the trip didn't work?" Carly asked. "You found out the identity of the other bidder."

"At what cost? I'm sorry. I know you had feelings for him. I...well, I didn't mean for things to get so muddled."

"Please," Carly said, waving her hand. "I was never interested in Josh. I mean, he's cute...but there's never been any spark. You know what I mean?"

Meredith swallowed her tea. "But the other day you told me you were worried that you might have feelings for him. That you might..."

"I have never felt anything for Josh. I just said that to get you to go out with him."

"What?"

"You've always liked him."

"What are you saying?"

"I'm saying it was all an act. Me pretending to be drunk and flirting with him. Threatening to call off the wedding."

"This was a fix-up?" The whole scene at the dining room table...the tears and accusations...had been an act? Meredith felt overcome with relief. *Carly had never liked Josh.*

Carly smiled proudly. "It was Mom's idea."

"Mom?"

Carly nodded. "She thought the whole scam up. I would pretend that I liked Josh to get you worried that he might be threatening the Durasnow deal. We knew it was the only way you'd agree to spend time with him."

Her mother and sister may have meant well, but their scheming had caused her quite a bit of trouble. "You shouldn't have made up that ridiculous story," Meredith said.

Carly leaned forward. "Please, don't be angry. We were just giving you an excuse to go for what you wanted."

Meredith sighed. "What would make you think I wanted Josh?"

Carly leaned back and shrugged. "Well, we all know what happened on Bear Mountain all those years ago."

"We do?" Could this get much worse?

"It's okay, Meredith. I mean, he's a really attractive guy who is obviously quite smitten with you."

"No, he's not," Meredith said.

"He must be. He slept with you."

Meredith took another sip of her tea. She inhaled the warm comforting scent of cinnamon. "He's always been a playboy." She sighed. "Josh and I do not have a future. We don't have anything in common…"

"Maybe not before. But you certainly do now. His company is huge, Meredith. He makes more money than you do. And his wealth isn't tied into stocks. He's liquid. He can buy things that we can't."

"Like Durasnow."

"Maybe. Maybe not."

Meredith hesitated. "There's more." She put down her teacup and said, "I accused him of coming back here to seduce you."

"What?"

"The first night I saw him, I even offered him money to leave you alone. The Durans got upset when they saw you dancing with him. And when Mother told me that you wanted to have one last fling, I panicked."

"Oh, dear, who knew I was such a good little actress?" Carly smiled, as if proud of herself. "Well, at least you know now that you were wrong. Josh's interest in me is strictly platonic. Maybe you should just call him up and tell him you're sorry…"

"Sorry?" Meredith stood and turned away from her sister. "He may not have been devious enough to break up your engagement, but he still lied to me. He pretended to be a ski instructor. I never would have…let things get so carried away if I had known he was the other bidder."

"Maybe it's a good thing he didn't tell you, then," Carly said.

Meredith turned back. "How can you say that?"

"Because...well, look at you. You're thirty-two years old. It's about time you got...busy."

"Busy?"

"You know what I mean."

"I'm not desperate," Meredith said.

"I'm not being critical," Carly said. "I think you're the most decent and moral person I know. But unfortunately, you're also lonely."

Meredith looked out the window. Light snow was falling. The world outside was beautiful, white and clean. "There's something about Josh," she said quietly. "Something that's different from any other man I've met."

"It's not hard to figure out. He's gorgeous and athletic. Charming and..."

"It's more than that," Meredith said. "It's a spark...a connection. I've met plenty of men over the years. But I haven't been tempted by any of them."

"You could do worse," Carly said.

"I don't know about that," Meredith said, shaking her head. "He's one of the bad boys we're so famous for choosing."

"Josh is a lot of things, but he's not bad."

"He's a playboy. A confirmed bachelor."

"And maybe you're just the woman to tame him."

"Carly," Meredith said carefully, turning from the window. "You do love Mark, don't you?"

"Of course. Why would you think otherwise?" Carly asked, though she wouldn't look Meredith in the eye.

"Josh thinks I'm forcing you into this marriage. Just so I can get my hands on Durasnow."

"That's ridiculous. No one can force me to do anything."

Meredith shrugged. "I wouldn't want you to marry anyone just to make me happy."

Carly stood and turned away. When she looked back, Meredith saw that her eyes were full of tears.

"I love him," she said, as if she was trying to convince herself. "At least, I think I do."

"You *think*…" The reality hit Meredith like a two-by-four across the back of her head. Josh was right. Carly did not want to marry Mark. And it was more than just last-minute jitters. Much more. "Oh, Carly," Meredith said as she crossed the room. She hugged her sister.

"I'm sorry, Meredith," Carly said. "I know I should be excited to marry such a wonderful guy, but something doesn't feel right."

"Call it off," Meredith said. "While there's still time."

"What will Mom say? And what about the company? You and I both know that my marrying Mark is the only way we're going to get Durasnow."

Meredith shook her head. "This is not a business deal. This is your future happiness. I'm not going to let you do something you don't want to do just to save the company."

"But—" Carly began.

"No." Meredith cut her off. "You can't. And quite frankly, your marrying Mark is *not* a guarantee that we'll get Durasnow. The Durans are still talking to Josh, aren't they?"

"But they haven't sold it to him," Carly said. "And they won't as long as I marry Mark."

"Maybe," Meredith said. "But maybe not."

"When are you going to see Josh again?"

"See him again?" Meredith swallowed. "Never, I hope."

"Tomorrow night is the masked ball. The Durans will be there. And so will Josh."

"How do you know Josh will be there?" Damn! Why did her heart quicken at the mere mention of his name?

"I'm sure of it," Carly said. "He's not going to leave Aspen until this deal is done."

"What does it matter?" Meredith said. "It's over. I don't want anything to do with him anymore."

"You have no choice," Carly said. "You have to try to work out a deal with him. I can't marry Mark, not like this. You have to give Josh a percentage of Durasnow."

Meredith knew what Carly was implying. She wanted the freedom to call off her engagement.

"You have to talk to Josh. And you have to do it soon."

"But once the engagement is called off, he'll have no reason to negotiate. He can just take all of Durasnow."

"Which is why you have to work fast. Get him to agree to share the company before he finds out Mark and I are breaking up."

Meredith knew Carly was right. But could she handle seeing Josh again? And how would she get him to agree to a merger?

"I'm not sure he'll go for it."

"Why not?" Carly asked.

"Because he offered already. And I turned him down."

"Well, you have to tell him you changed your mind."

"He'll never believe that. He'll know something is up."

Carly smiled. "You'll figure out a way. When you see him, act as casual as possible. Get him to bring up Durasnow and then tell him you've reconsidered his offer. You want to bury the hatchet."

"Bury the hatchet?"

"Whatever. You have to get an agreement before word of my breakup with Mark hits the papers."

"When are you going to talk to Mark?"

"As soon as he gets back. The day after the ball."

Meredith nodded. She sighed. "I don't like the idea of tricking Josh into a deal."

"This is business," Carly said.

"This is not going to be easy."

"You're going to use all of your charms."

"I need more than that," Meredith said. "I need some magic that will make him forget everything I said."

Carly smiled. "Leave it all to me."

Josh leaned back in his chair and looked around the hotel suite that had become his makeshift office. He raked his fingers through his hair and spun around from his computer, unable to concentrate.

In fact, since he had last seen Meredith, he couldn't seem to do anything at all.

How dare she accuse him of planning to seduce Carly...just to get a business deal? He would never play with another person's emotions like that.

Unlike Meredith.

You were a flirtation that needed to be dealt with...

He realized that both of his fists were clenched. Opening his hands, he tilted his neck from side to side, attempting to relax.

What was wrong with him? Women did not typically

have this effect upon him. Why was Meredith different? After all, they had only made love. It was a little bit of sex. Nothing more.

But what an experience! Once again, he felt a ripple of excitement as he remembered the way it had felt to be inside Meredith, exploring her, feeling her as no man had done before. She was his, only his.

There had been something in her eyes. An innocence. The tough, corporate, iron-maiden strategist had become a sweet, simple woman more than capable of giving and receiving sensual love.

Not that he cared, of course. *Not that he cared.*

But hell…he did care. More than he wanted to admit.

He glanced at the offer in front of him. He was doubling his last bid. It was twice as much money as Durasnow was worth. But he didn't care. It would put an end to this ridiculous competition with Cartwright Enterprises. He was certain the Durans, regardless of Carly's engagement, would accept. After all, they would be foolish to turn it down. No other company would be willing or able to match it, including Cartwright.

Josh could return to Switzerland with the product he wanted. And he could go about his life, just as before.

So why, he thought, hadn't he sent the offer?

His official excuse was that the Durans had been out of town. He preferred to present his final offers in person so that both parties were able to sign and seal the deal on the spot.

But that was not the real reason. After all, the Durans had returned this morning and the offer was still sitting on his desk.

He was hesitating because he knew the impact this would have on Cartwright Enterprises. And he was holding out hope that Meredith might come to her senses. The only way she could keep her job and the company she loved would be to negotiate with him. They would have to become partners.

But Meredith had not attempted to contact him since they'd returned two days ago. And it was looking as though she never would.

So he owed her nothing. He had given her two days to reconsider. That was more than generous. He was fighting fair and square. It was a simple business deal. What did he care if Cartwright Enterprises lost Durasnow?

But he did. As much as he hated to admit it, he felt protective of Meredith. She needed this deal. And despite his better instincts, he wanted to help her.

There might be one last opportunity for fate to intervene.

He leaned forward and sighed. The winter ball was tonight. Everyone in Aspen, including the Durans, would be in attendance. And surely so would Meredith.

The possibility of seeing her again made his heart race.

He would wait until after the ball to make his offer. He would try to talk to Meredith one more time.

It was against his better instincts. But he had no choice. For once, his heart was overruling his mind.

Eight

Meredith entered the Rosewood Ballroom at exactly ten minutes before nine. The butterflies swirling around her belly had almost caused her to turn back twice on the way here. If it hadn't been for Carly, she would have. But the fact that her sister—who was about to endure something much worse than a simple business negotiation—was so cool and composed, shamed her into submission.

"Are you okay?" she asked Carly.

"I'm fine. I'll be better after I talk to Mark."

"I know."

Carly glanced at her. "Don't do that."

"Do what?"

"That thing you do when you're nervous. Bite your bottom lip like that. You'll smear your lipstick."

"Oh," Meredith said. "Right." Damn the lipstick.

Normally, she didn't wear any makeup but tonight she'd made an exception. She was dressed in a long, strapless black gown that clung to her in all the right places. Her hair was swept off her shoulders, wrapped in a loose chignon. And her makeup had been professionally applied. She felt stiff and unnatural, which only added to her discomfort.

"Don't be nervous," Carly said. "It's just business, remember?"

That, unfortunately, was the problem. It was just business, but her heart wouldn't let her forget her feelings for Josh were far from professional. However, she was not about to clutter her sister's overwhelmed mind with her own insignificant complaints. Carly had enough on her shoulders.

"Do you see him?" Carly asked, leaning against her.

Meredith held the mask to her face as she scanned the crowd. Most of the guests were wearing masks, so it was not difficult to spot Josh. He, once again, had gone against tradition. Although he was attired in the obligatory tuxedo, he had not donned a mask.

He was talking to a blonde who had her mask pulled up on her forehead, as if to give Josh a better view of her lovely face. And from the looks of it, her ploy seemed to be working. Josh was leaning forward, looking at her intently.

"He's busy," Meredith said.

Carly glanced at Josh and then back at Meredith. "You're not jealous, are you?" she asked with a coy smile.

"Of course not," Meredith said.

Carly gave her an understanding, almost maternal look. As if she was saying, *Suu-uuure, you're not!*

"You have to go interrupt him," Carly instructed. "Flirt a little. Talk to him."

Meredith glanced across the room. Josh was now slow dancing with the glamorous-looking blonde, his hand resting against her back.

"And you're going to have to do it now," Carly said. "Because my future ex-in-laws have spotted me." Meredith glanced behind her. The Durans were waving at Carly, motioning for her to join them.

Meredith heard Carly breathe a long, deep sigh. Forgetting all about her troubles, and once again focused on her sister, she gave Carly a hug. "It'll be okay," she told her, "whatever you decide."

"I know," Carly said, doing her best to smile. "Now go."

Meredith took several steps and stopped. She didn't know how she was going to approach Josh, what she was going to say. She needed more time. Just as she was trying to figure a way out of the ballroom, a voice behind her said, "Hello, Meredith."

It was not Josh, but Frank Cummings, a man she had known for years. He was a local dentist and had at times acted as her emergency date.

She forced a smile. "How are you, Frank?"

"Fine thanks. How are *you?* I heard about your ski accident."

"I'm doing well. Luckily, my sprain is feeling much better. Frank," she said quickly. "Would you like to dance?"

After extracting himself from the toothy blonde, Josh moved to a corner of the ballroom and watched as a man approached Meredith with a certain look in his eyes. He knew the look. And he didn't appreciate it.

Damn. He was jealous. Once again he reprimanded himself for letting his emotions get the best of him.

Unable to tear his eyes away, Josh watched as Meredith moved onto the dance floor with the man and rested her head against his lapel.

He had made a mistake. He should've given the Durans his offer immediately upon his return. He should've closed the deal and left town. He could be home in Switzerland right now, taking care of business.

His hand tightened into a fist as he saw the man rest his palm on Meredith's rear.

Keep your hands off her.

Josh made his way through the crowd, not hearing the greetings from old friends as he passed. His mind was focused on his objective.

"Excuse me," he said, tapping Meredith's dance partner on the shoulder. "Mind if I interrupt?"

Meredith turned around, her jaw dropping slightly in surprise.

"Well, Josh, how are you? Frank Cummings, remember me?" Frank asked.

"Of course I do," Josh said, towering over Frank. "And how are you?"

Frank laughed. "Great. Business couldn't be better. So I hear you're still giving those private lessons on Bear Mountain."

Josh stared at Meredith. What had she told Frank? "Only for those willing to pay the price."

Frank laughed.

"Excuse me," Josh said. He slid his arm around Meredith's waist before either she or Frank had a chance to object and danced her away from the other man.

Meredith handled the interruption with the composure she was famous for. Without skipping a beat she said, "You're not wearing a mask."

"Neither are you."

"I'm holding mine." She glanced around. "What happened to your date?"

"What date?"

"The woman you were dancing with. The blonde."

"I have no idea. I've never seen her before and I doubt I'll ever see her again."

"Oh," she replied. She was feigning nonchalance, but there was something else. Could it be relief?

"Thank you for sending me my backpack," she said.

"My pleasure," he replied. He nodded toward her ankle. "I see you're feeling better."

"Almost good as new," she said. "It's amazing what a change of scenery will do."

"True."

"Speaking of which," she said. "I'm surprised your scenery hasn't changed."

Damn, she was beautiful. "I'm not ready to leave," he said. "I still have some unfinished business in Aspen."

"I was a bit surprised you haven't countered our offer yet."

She was acting as if they had parted on the most polite of terms. The animosity and anger was gone. Or was it?

Josh stopped dancing. "I want to talk to you."

Meredith nodded. She met his gaze directly and said, "And I want to talk to you."

His lips curled up in a half smile. "You do, do you?" he said.

Meredith had seen that look before. It was the same, hazy, full-of-sex look he had given her right after they had made love. Meredith could feel the heat seeping up her cheeks.

She hesitated. *Play it cool.*

"What a coincidence," he said. He took her arm and steered her into the lobby. Several times they met old friends who tried to talk to Josh, but he brushed them off, his hand never leaving her arm.

"Josh," she said, nodding toward his hand. "You don't have to worry about me escaping down the mountain anymore."

"Sorry," Josh said, dropping his hand.

Immediately she regretted her words. What was wrong with his hand on her arm? But she couldn't stand it. It was too intimate. It made her feel...as if she belonged to him.

Josh glanced inside the crowded bar, then shook his head. "We can't talk in here. There are too many people we know." He turned toward the lobby. "I know a place. Follow me." He headed toward the elevators.

"Where are we going?" she asked.

"My room."

She stopped in her tracks. "Your room?"

"Get your mind out of the gutter," Josh said. "It's a suite. I've been conducting business out of it all week."

"I bet you have."

"Not that kind of business," he said, stepping inside the elevator.

"Not that it's any of *my* business," she said.

Josh winked. "Whatever you say, Princess. Just keep

your hands to yourself. We're being watched." He nodded toward the security cameras mounted in the elevator and pressed the button for the penthouse.

"Please don't call me Princess. It's annoying."

"All right, Ms. Cartwright."

The elevator stopped at the top floor. The doors opened onto a grand, almost garish room. It looked, Meredith thought, like a boudoir from the eighteen hundreds.

"Here we are," he said. "Home sweet home, at least for now."

"Who's the decorator? Brothels Are Us?" she asked, following him inside.

"Fortunately, I had nothing to do with the furnishings. I am, however, responsible for the mess." He nodded toward the stacks of paper cluttering the room.

She stepped over a mound of paperwork and headed toward the giant picture window. She stopped short when she recognized Bear Mountain in the distance.

She turned away. She would never look at Bear Mountain again without being reminded of the intimacy she and Josh had shared.

Josh was looking at her carefully. After a pause, he asked, "What did you want to talk to me about?"

She swallowed before replying, "I've been thinking about your offer. About combining forces."

He walked over to the window and closed the drapes. "Why the change of heart?"

"I've had a chance to step back. To think it over."

"And time alone was enough to make you reconsider?"

He was not buying her excuse. *Keep trying,* she told herself. "I think I let my personal feelings get in the way of what was best for the company."

He paused, staring at her. "You were pretty adamant about getting it yourself."

"Like I said, I've had a chance to reconsider."

"What's going on, Meredith? Did Carly take up with someone else while you were out distracting me?"

How dare he? Yet, he was not too far off the mark. Carly may not have taken up with someone else, but her engagement was about to be called off. She turned back toward the elevator. "I've made a mistake."

"Sit down," he said in a tone that demanded obedience. In spite of herself, she sat on the sofa.

Looking at her, he seemed to soften. "Can I get you a drink?"

"Okay," she said. Perhaps a drink might help to quiet her nerves.

He walked over to the liquor cabinet, poured them both a brandy, then moved to the sofa and handed her a glass. She took a sip. The liquid burned as it slid down her throat, settling in her belly. She coughed.

"Easy there," he said.

She held her fist to her chest and coughed again. "I'm fine."

He nodded. She could tell he was suppressing a smile. He held the glass to his lips, drinking the brandy as if it was water. When he was finished, he said, "I wanted to apologize again for not telling you who I was before. I'm sorry I...well, took advantage of the situation on Bear Mountain." He drained his glass.

"Apology accepted," she said. Very good, she commended herself. Now they were on more friendly terms.

"Let me ask you something," he said. "If we were to...join forces, so to speak, do you think we would be able to deal with each other on a professional level?"

"Of course."

"Even with our...well, history?"

She smiled politely. "What history?"

"Okay," he said, but whatever warmth had been in his voice was gone. "Sixty-forty. I keep the majority."

She leaned back on the sofa, breathing a sigh of relief. The offer was still on the table. And she hadn't even needed to beg. She laughed. "Absolutely not."

"You're making a mistake."

"Your first offer was more generous."

"My next one will be even less so."

"I'll just buy it myself." It was time to play hardball. Let him think she still had the upper hand. "After all, it really should stay in the family." She stood and walked toward the elevator. "I apologize for wasting your time."

She pressed the button for the elevator, and he was behind her before she knew it. He leaned over her, and whispered in her ear, "Don't be a fool, Meredith. You know you'll never win a bidding war with me. I know all about you, all about the problems you've been having at Cartwright. You need this. I know it, you know it, your stockholders know it. And you don't stand a chance in hell of getting it."

"Carly is marrying the Durans' son. They'd never do anything to upset Mark."

"Do you honestly think they prize familial connections over money?" He paused, his eyes sweeping over her face. "What about you, Meredith? Would you let your heart get in the way of a business deal?"

He was too close. Way too close. She glanced at his lips, remembering how they felt.

Her mind had stopped working. She had forgotten all about the strategy she had worked out with Carly.

All she could think about was how much she wanted to kiss Josh. She could almost feel his arms around her, his fingers touching and caressing…

She needed to get out of here. Quick.

The elevator door opened. Meredith practically fell backward, escaping inside.

Josh held the door, stopping it from closing. "Why are you running away?"

"I'm not."

He hesitated, a look of surprise crossing his face. "You're still afraid of me, aren't you?"

Meredith's heart stopped. Afraid? Yes! Yes, of course she was afraid. She couldn't be in the same room with him for one minute without remembering their night together. Without craving his touch.

He was in front of her now, his one hand grazing her cheek. "Why?" he said.

She swallowed. His hand felt so good. She closed her eyes. *Stay strong. Do not give in to temptation.*

"Don't leave," he said. His mouth was against her, his lips brushing her cheek. "Stay."

"I can't," she said. *Go,* her mind screamed. *Run.*

"All right," he said. He nodded. "I just have one question for you, then I'll let you go."

She could handle one question. "Okay."

"Why did you make love to me on the mountain?"

"As you said yourself, things got…out of hand."

"Were you telling me the truth when you said I was the only man you've ever slept with?"

"Yes."

"Why?"

"You've asked more than one question," she said. She pressed the button to close the elevator door.

"Why did you wait for me, Meredith?"

His question caught her by surprise. For a second she couldn't speak. Wait…for him? Had she been waiting for him?

"I wasn't," she said. "The situation just…well, it never presented itself."

"I find it hard to believe that no man has wanted you." His gaze shifted. His eyes took their time, pausing on her breasts, working their way down her legs. It was as if he was drinking her in, caressing her with his eyes. "You're a beautiful woman."

"Please stop," she said.

His eyes met hers. "You need me, Meredith."

Did he mean personally or professionally? If he meant professionally, he was right. She couldn't leave without an agreement. Regardless of how uncomfortable she was.

She stepped out of the elevator. "Okay," she said quietly. The door closed behind her.

"Okay what?"

"I'll think about your offer."

He hesitated, obviously disappointed that they were once again talking business. But he didn't skip a beat. "Ah," he said. "Back to that, are we?" He crossed his arms and said, "I want an answer tonight."

"I can't give you an answer tonight. I have to run it past the board."

"No, you don't. Since when do you listen to anyone, anyway?"

"If I'm not going to run it past the board, you have

to sweeten it. It has to be an offer of which I'm certain they'll approve. Fifty-fifty.''

He crossed his arms in front of him. She could see a grin forming on the corner of his lips. ''You drive a hard bargain.''

''Take it or leave it.''

He paused, letting his eyes gaze over her once again. ''I'll take it.''

Meredith breathed a sigh of relief. There. She had done it. Now she was free to leave. So why did she feel unable to move?

He obviously had no intention of moving, either. He stood still, his face close to hers.

''I should go,'' she whispered.

''Goodbye,'' he said. The elevator button was just to her right. But for some reason she couldn't lift her hand.

His breath touched her first. His lips followed, brushing across her forehead, moving toward her cheek. His finger touched her neck, tracing an imaginary line down and around the top of her dress.

''I...I really need to get back.''

''Go ahead,'' he replied. He cupped her face in his hands. His lips touched hers. His mouth explored tentatively at first, then with enough passion and force to take her breath away. She could feel the tingle all the way down her spine.

''What are you doing?'' she murmured.

''I'm kissing you, Meredith,'' he said softly.

He kissed her again. This time her hands reached around his neck, pulling him toward her. ''Stay with me tonight,'' he whispered as he kissed her ear.

''I can't,'' she said. ''My sister...''

''Leave your cell on.'' He took her hands and held

them firmly in his. He kissed her neck. "If she's worried, she'll call."

She was no longer thinking. Her mind was frozen.

But her feet were moving. And they were moving toward him, following him into the bedroom.

She stopped at the foot of the bed. Silently Josh walked behind her to unzip her gown. She stood still as her dress fell to the floor, and then she was clad only in black lace panties and stiletto heels. Josh pulled her back against him, ran his hands up and down her body, as if committing it to memory. He hooked his fingers inside her panties and pulled them down over her shoes.

After she kicked off her panties, he spun her around so that she was facing him.

He was still completely dressed in his tuxedo but she didn't bother removing his clothes. Looking into his eyes, she unzipped his pants and reached for him, wrapping her fingers around his aroused length.

He closed his eyes and leaned into her. She had turned the tables, she was in control. His eyes grew smaller, his breath ragged. It was more exciting than she had imagined. She had never done such a thing.

But she was not satisfied with just a touch. Kneeling in front of him, she ran her tongue around him, taking him deep within her mouth. She explored him much as he had her, depending on instinct for instruction. His moans were more stimulating than she had ever imagined.

All she cared about was giving him pleasure. His hands raked through her hair. It was not the soft, gentle touch she had enjoyed earlier, but the rough, passionate feel of a man who was no longer thinking with reason.

He needed her, just as she needed him.

He lifted her up, placing her on the edge of the bed, still kneeling but facing away from him. He put himself inside her and began thrusting in and out. This was not the tender lovemaking they had enjoyed on the mountainside, but wild, uninhibited passion.

The world spun and her body continued to respond. She was in control and desperate at the same time, reacting and moving by instinct.

It was as if they were the only two people on earth. As if this was the reason she had been born, just for this moment. Nothing else mattered. Nothing else would ever matter.

Release came with a thunder. She fell forward onto the bed, holding herself up as her body pulsed with pleasure.

Afterward, he took her into his arms, and she realized she did not feel uncomfortable by her nakedness. She liked the feel of his tuxedo against her bare skin. She liked the way he held her, strongly and possessively. It was as if he was saying, *You're mine. You belong to me.*

She felt like a woman, a feminine and sensual being.

He reached out a hand and touched her cheek. "So, can I take this as a yes?"

"What?"

"Partners?"

Oh, what the hell. She hugged him. "Partners."

He smiled. "This will mean we'll have to be seeing quite a bit of each other."

"I don't know," she said, motioning toward her naked body, "if there's much more to see."

He laughed. It was a hearty, relaxed sound. He picked up a tendril of hair that had fallen out of her chignon and tenderly hooked it behind her ear. "You're full of surprises, Ms. Cartwright.'' He ran his finger around her lips. ''Are you hungry?''

She realized she hadn't eaten anything all day. Her nerves had gotten the best of her. Suddenly, she was starving. She nodded.

''Good,'' he said. He grabbed her dress off the floor. ''Why don't you put this back on. I know exactly where I want to take you.''

''We're going out?'' she asked, pulling her dress back on.

''Not exactly,'' he said, a devilish smile crossing his lips. ''I just didn't want you to get cold.''

He picked up the phone. ''Do you like lobster?'' he asked.

She nodded and turned toward the mirror. As he ordered champagne and lobsters from room service, she attempted to fix her hair. It was hopeless. She looked exactly like she was: a woman who had just made mad, passionate love.

Josh hung up the phone. He looked at Meredith's reflection in the mirror. She was the most beautiful woman he had ever seen. After a while, he walked to stand behind her, sliding his hands around her waist. ''I'm a mess,'' she said.

''On the contrary,'' he said. He pulled her around so that she was facing him. ''I've never seen a woman look so ravishing.''

She smiled. ''Tell me about you...about your life in Switzerland.''

''I think you'd like it there. Some of it is very historical...cobblestone streets and old-fashioned villages. But Zurich is very cosmopolitan.''

"That's where you live?"

He nodded. "I have an apartment in Zurich and a country house in a little mountain village."

"So you have the best of both worlds."

"I prefer the country. In Zurich I live in the same building where my office is."

"You've come a long way."

He took her hands. "Thanks, in part, to you."

"To me?"

He nodded. "You were my motivation."

"I don't understand."

"All those years ago, when I tried to call you and it became apparent you didn't want anything to do with me...well, I knew that you would never be interested in someone like me."

"That wasn't true," she said. "I told you, I was just nervous. I had a terrible crush on you."

"Still, the truth of the matter was that I was a playboy with no direction. What could I offer a smart girl with a brilliant future?"

"I'm surprised you cared. After all, you had plenty of girls..."

"Not the kind of girls I wanted. I wanted someone... like you."

"I'm sure you meet all types of women now."

There *were* other women in his life. But how could he return to them now that he had been with Meredith? He doubted he could ever find a woman who would compare.

Before he could answer, they were interrupted by a knock on the door. "That was fast," she said, breaking away.

Too fast. Josh was not ready for their dinner to arrive.

He was enjoying his conversation with Meredith. But, he reminded himself, there would be other opportunities. Now that the Durasnow business was settled, he could focus on his personal agenda: getting to know Meredith.

While Meredith went into the bathroom to fix her hair, Josh had the waiter set up their meal in the intimate dining room.

After the waiter had left, Meredith stepped out of the bathroom and smiled at the table that had been set so romantically.

Meredith waited as Josh pulled out a chair for her. When she was settled, he popped open the champagne and poured them each a glass.

"To partnership," he said, raising his glass.

Meredith touched her glass to his. But a veil of caution had slid over her eyes. She may have been sitting across from him but her mind seemed a million miles away.

"You did the right thing, Meredith," he said. "By joining forces with me you've saved your company."

Once again, Meredith glanced away. "I'd like to see Switzerland one day," she said wistfully.

"I would like that, too," he said, smiling.

They ate in silence. But it was the comfortable, intimate silence of lovers. Afterward, he took her hand and led her outside to the edge of the balcony.

"This is strange," she said, putting her hands on the railing. "Staring out at Bear Mountain.

He put his arms around her waist and held her to him. He thought of what Meredith had said about visiting Switzerland. Perhaps she was also feeling the connection between them. "That's where we spent the night," he said, pointing over her shoulder to a spot on the mountain.

She twisted around in his arms. "You're cold," she said, slipping her hands around his waist. He glanced down. Her dress had fallen slightly. He could see her nipples peeking out of the top. The effect on him was immediate. The dress had to go.

He glanced over at the hot tub where the water bubbled—hot and ready. "I can think of one way to warm up."

He took her hand and led her over to the tub where he unzipped her dress. Kicking off her shoes, she stepped naked into the water and sat on the inside ledge. Her firm, high breasts bobbed on top of the water.

He swallowed.

"Care to join me?" she asked.

He kicked off his shoes and clothes, then slid in next to her. He put his arm around her and kissed her shoulder.

Meredith looked up at him and raised her slender hand to his cheek.

"This feels like a dream," she said.

"But it's real."

"What are you thinking?" she asked.

"I'm thinking there's no place I'd rather be than here with you."

She pushed herself up and sat on his lap, facing him. She reached under the water and found him, led him inside. The warm, churning water bubbled and popped as she began moving up and down, all the while staring into his eyes.

It was the most intimate sexual encounter he had ever

experienced. He leaned back, watching her pleasure herself.

She moaned slightly and paused. He could tell she was attempting to stall her release. He wanted to help her. To make her feel good…to give her the same gratification she gave him.

He held on to her hips, raising her up. ''Wait,'' he said. ''Not yet. Just breathe.''

She closed her eyes. He watched her breathe slowly, her chest expanding with each labored breath. He could tell the immediate need for release was subsiding. ''That's it,'' he said softly, like a patient teacher. He put her back on top of him, arching his back so that he could penetrate her more deeply.

He raised her up and lowered her carefully back down. He let it build slowly, taking his time, enjoying each and every thrust.

''Please,'' she said. He could see the desperation in her eyes. She dug her fingernails into his arm. ''Please let me go.''

He waited and then began to move with force. As she began her release, she nestled her head in his shoulder to quiet her scream of pleasure.

Only when she was almost done did he allow himself to follow.

Nine

They made love several more times that night, getting precious few hours of sleep. But the next morning, Meredith woke feeling refreshed and well-rested.

"What are you thinking about?" Josh leaned over her, his finger tracing her lips. He was naked, each muscle on his strong torso clearly defined in the daylight.

"You," she said.

He picked up her hand and kissed it. "I want you to stay with me today."

She shook her head. "I've got to go to work..."

"Let Carly handle it."

She smiled. "Carly doesn't do much there. I mean, she has an office but I don't even think she knows where it is."

"She doesn't need to. You take care of everything." He kissed her hand and said, "She'll find her way."

Meredith sighed. She would like nothing better than to stay with Josh but she had missed enough time from the office. She needed to get back. And she needed to break the news to her mother that the Durasnow rights were going to be shared. And worse, she needed to console her mother when she discovered Carly was not going to marry Mark.

Josh put his hands behind his head and leaned back on the pillows. "Besides," he said. "We need to hammer out our deal."

She stiffened slightly. "It's fifty-fifty, right?"

"That's what we agreed to." He smiled and shook his head. "You don't trust me at all, do you?"

"What is there to hammer out?"

"It's an excuse, Meredith. I'm giving you an excuse to miss work. I'll write you a note if you like."

"I'm sorry," she said. "I just, well, I just think we should be careful."

"Careful?"

"That our affair doesn't get...complicated." She couldn't handle dealing with a bout of unrequited love. She had known the score from the beginning. This was to be a business deal with a little pleasure mixed in. Some people played golf with their business associates. She and Josh made love.

See, Meredith? she said silently. *It's really quite simple. Not complicated at all.*

"Of course," he said, dropping his arms. "And would spending another day with me complicate things for you?"

Because, he might as well have said, *it certainly wouldn't complicate anything for me.*

"No." She smiled again. "I just wanted to make sure we're still on the same page."

"I.e., you want to make sure I'm not falling in love with you."

She held her breath. She couldn't bear to hear him say that he wasn't. That he would never love someone like her.

He smiled. But it was not the mischievous smile she had seen so often. It was a forced smile, slightly sad. "I'm leaving to go back to Europe soon," he said. "I'd like to spend time with you while I still can."

Her heart sank at the thought of him leaving. It would not be easy to say goodbye.

But still…she wasn't ready to leave. "Okay," she said.

He pulled her back into his arms. "Okay what?"

"I'm yours for today."

He kissed her once again.

"But," she said, "first I have to go home and change."

"I'll have clothes sent up for you from the boutique downstairs."

"Apparently you've had experience with this sort of situation."

He kissed her. "No experience has prepared me for someone like you."

"I have to call my office," she said, smiling. "Then I'm all yours."

"All right," he said. "But don't tell anyone about our partnership yet."

"Why not?"

"Because I think we need to talk to the Durans first. Together. Present a united front."

"But we've been bidding against each other."

"We're about to stop. Let them wonder what's going on. We're in the driver's seat now."

It made sense. But could she trust him not to make another solo bid?

As if reading her mind, he looked her in the eye and said, "Trust me." Getting out of bed, he picked up his cell phone. "Look, I'm turning my phone off. Let's forget about business and spend the day with each other." He picked up her purse and handed it to her. "What do you say?"

She hesitated, before reaching into her purse and pulling out her phone. What did she have to lose? Besides, of course, her company, her career and her heart? "I have to call my sister, though. Let her know that I'm all right." That she was better than all right. That she was great. Terrific.

She dialed Carly's cell number but she didn't pick up. Rather than try her at home and risk the chance of reaching her mother instead, she left a message.

This is ridiculous, she realized. *I'm actually nervous about telling my mother I spent the night with a man. And no regular guy, either. Josh. Mr. Playboy. Mr. Durasnow rival.*

When she finished, she held up her phone so that Josh could see her turn it off.

"How do you feel?" he asked.

"Naked."

"You are naked," he said. His eyes shone with the mischievous twinkle she had begun to recognize. "I'll have to think of some creative way to distract you." He took her phone out of her hand and placed it on the bedside table. "The first hour is always the hardest." He leaned over and kissed her on the neck.

"I knew," she said, "I could count on you."

Josh put on his turn signal and glanced at Meredith. At her request, he had kept the car's roof down. Meredith was obviously enjoying the fresh air. She was leaning back in the seat, her long hair blowing in the wind.

She saw him looking at her and smiled. "I think I know where we're going. You're interested in the Algiers Hotel, aren't you?"

He smiled. He had known from the moment they'd decided to spend the day together where he wanted to take her.

In the nineteen-sixties and seventies the Algiers was one of the premiere hotels in the world. By the eighties, however, it had started to fall into disrepair. It closed in the early nineties and was used for a while as a nursing home. It had been empty for the past five years.

"Right as usual," he said.

Josh had once thought about buying the old Algiers Hotel. At the time he had rejected it. It had been empty for years and would cost millions to renovate. Besides that, his business was in Europe. He was not looking to expand in the States.

So why was he taking another look? Why, all of a sudden, did an expansion seem to make perfect sense?

"Are you interested in it?"

"Maybe. It's where my aunt used to work," he said. "In fact, I used to work there as a kid, as well."

"Really?"

"Sure. I was a bellboy. I couldn't stand it though. I hated being inside."

''So,'' she said, ''you're thinking about expanding into the U.S.?''

Josh couldn't help but notice the lack of enthusiasm in her voice. But what was he expecting? She had been clear about her feelings. He shrugged. ''Who knows?''

Meredith felt a surge of excitement. Josh was thinking about buying the Algiers! That meant more opportunities to be with him. Perhaps their relationship would be more than just a one-night stand...or two-night, as the case might be.

Don't, she warned herself. Josh was not the settling-down type. He knew it, she knew it.

''I looked into buying this hotel at one time, myself,'' she said, as Josh pulled into the empty hotel parking lot.

''I know you did.''

''How did you know that?''

''I know a lot of things about you. I've been following your career for years.''

She smiled. ''Do you know why I passed on it?''

''I was hoping you might tell me.''

''I think it has a lot of potential, but it needs someone who's willing and able to sink a lot of money into it. And not just the building. The mountain needs some help, too. Trails need to be cut. There could be a few more beginner slopes, as well. Make it more accessible to those people who are not as intense about skiing.''

He laughed. ''Like you?''

''Exactly.'' She smiled.

He took her hand and led her around back. They walked in through a screened porch. ''My aunt used to wait tables out here in the summer.'' He pointed to the small practice golf range. "I once got picked up for trespassing for playing that range at night."

"Trespassing?"

"That was the least of my offenses here."

"I bet. These waitresses were known as the pretty ones in town."

He grinned, took her hand and led her into the hotel's cavernous foyer. He stood behind her, his arms wrapped around her waist. "I used to come here a lot at night. I spent hours sitting in the big, overstuffed chairs they had by the fire."

"What did you think about?"

"I'd think about what it might be like to be rich. And I thought, One day I'm going to own this place." He spun her around so that he could look at her. "What about you? What was your dream as a child?"

"My dream?" She laughed. "I had a couple."

"Of course. I didn't think you'd be happy or satisfied with just one," he said, teasing.

"I wanted to be the most powerful woman in the world."

"Naturally."

"I don't mean president or anything like that. I just meant I didn't want to be beholden to anyone. I wanted to be the master of my own destiny."

"Aren't we all?"

"It didn't feel like that to me. I felt like my stepfather was so controlling. I was always trying so hard to impress him. But it never seemed to work."

"I remember your stepdad well. At one point he asked me to stay away from you."

"He did? What would make him think that you were interested in me?"

"I think," he said, "he thought that you were inter-ested in me. And he didn't think I could or would turn you away. And he was right."

"Well, he was perceptive."

He laughed. It was a big, rich sound, as if he really were delighted. "What was your other dream?"

"I think what every girl dreams of. A fairy-tale love. White knight in shining armor. That sort of thing."

"Yet you avoid love."

She stood back. "I don't know about that. Maybe I'm waiting for the right person." She sneaked a peek at him. "Not that you're one to talk."

"What does that mean? You think I avoid love?"

"Don't you?"

He put his hands on her shoulders. "Maybe I'm wait-ing, too." He touched her cheek. After a pause, he smiled and took her hand, leading her to the stairs. "Want to see the penthouse?" he asked. "I've never been up there before."

"Let's go," Meredith said, leading the way.

He followed, enjoying the way her hips swayed se-ductively as she climbed the stairs. She reached the top and paused, waiting for him. Josh stepped past her and opened the door.

As with everything else in the building, the rooms were bare, covered in years of dust. But one could still sense an aura of grandeur, of what once was.

"It would make a nice apartment," she said.

Josh couldn't help reading sentiment into her state-ment. Was she insinuating that he could use it for per-sonal quarters? Did she want him to live here?

He led her over to the picture windows. Once again

Josh found himself overlooking Bear Mountain, this time from the opposite side.

"Well?" he said, watching Meredith. "Have you seen enough?"

"Yes," she replied, smiling. "I think you should buy it."

"Are you sure?" he asked. "I'd need to oversee the renovations. And I wouldn't want to own just one hotel in the States. I'd have to expand my entire operations."

"So?"

"That would mean I'd be back here a lot. I wouldn't want to cramp your style."

"I don't think eating dinner by myself at the office is exactly a style you can cramp."

"Maybe you wouldn't be eating by yourself."

"We'll see," she said.

He pulled her to him. "Blowing me off again, Princess?"

She withdrew her hand from his. "Nope. And as I said, I'm not a princess. And this is no fairy tale."

"How do you know?"

"Josh, I know how this works. I act disenchanted, you're interested. But the minute I start actually caring about you, you're out of here."

That might be how he'd behaved in the past, but this was different. Meredith was different.

"Maybe," he said, "I just hadn't found someone like you."

He heard himself say the words, but he couldn't quite believe they had come out of his mouth. Meredith appeared as stunned as Josh.

Meredith was watching him carefully. "I wasn't fishing for a compliment."

Josh didn't know what to say. He wanted to persuade Meredith to trust him. But was he worthy of her trust?

"Don't worry, Josh," she said. "I'm not going to hold you to it." She glanced at her watch. "I really should check my messages."

"No," he said, taking her hand. "We made a deal. One day with no phones, no office. Just us."

She smiled, though it seemed tinged with sadness. "As my mother just said to me, 'If I didn't know better, I'd think you were a romantic.'"

It was his turn to smile. "You have no idea."

Meredith thought for a moment. "Do you think you'll ever be anything but a serial philanderer?"

She could see him visibly stiffen. "That's what you think of me?"

Immediately she felt bad for insulting him. "I'm sorry," she said. "I'm out of line."

But the damage had already been done. "Why don't you come right out and ask me, Meredith?"

"Ask what?"

"Ask me if I'm going to fall into bed with another woman the minute I leave you."

"I don't have to ask," she said. "I know you."

"You *knew* me." He sighed. "Look, I can't believe we're even having this conversation, but here it goes. You knew me years ago. I was a kid. True, I had my share of women. I couldn't quite tell the difference between lust and love. But I've grown up. I know the difference now. And although I still enjoy sex and women, I would like nothing better to settle down with one woman."

"You'd get bored."

"On the contrary, I think it would be extremely exciting. Does that change your opinion of me?"

She shrugged.

"Believe it or not, it's true," he said. "But I can't rush it. When it's right, I'll know."

She couldn't help but take offense at his words. *When it's right, I'll know.* What was he saying? That it was obviously not right with her? She was obviously not the one?

So what? Why should she care?

Because at that moment she wanted nothing more than to be the one who captured Josh Adams's heart. "Good for you," she said.

"What about you?" he asked. "Would you like to get married one day?"

"Are you proposing?" she joked. It was one of those jokes that fell out of her mouth before she had a chance to stop it. She winced, anticipating his reaction. Perhaps just a scream and a run for the hills?

But he wasn't running. He was looking at her. It was an intense, searing look, a look that meant there was a lot riding on the right response.

He took her hand in his. "I don't want to frighten you."

She swallowed. "Scare away."

"Okay." He kissed her hand and said, "I can't remember ever feeling this way about someone."

"Me?" She couldn't breathe. Could it be? Did he really care about her?

He kissed her hand again. "I care about you, Meredith... In fact, I'm beginning to think that maybe I've been waiting for...for you."

Meredith's heart was beating so loudly she was certain

he could hear. Yet only one thing was important. "Kiss me, Josh."

Within a second her jacket was unzipped. She felt Josh's hands against her bare breasts. This is all that mattered, she told herself. The physical. The here and now. She couldn't worry about a future she knew would never happen.

What mattered was now.

He touched her nipple.

This was what was real.

She lay on the floor, taking him with her. She needed to feel him inside her. To know that everything was all right.

He was all around her, consuming her senses. He was all she needed. Now and forever. She would live this moment as if it were her last. She would give him everything she had and more.

They moved separately and together, each anticipating the other's needs and desires. And as the familiar explosion of pleasure rocked her, she thought only of Josh, concentrating on the physical connection with the man whom…the man whom she could love.

As they drove back to Josh's hotel, Meredith wondered if her life would ever be the same. Now that she'd had a taste of what having Josh in her life could be like, could she be happy without him?

She thought of the impending holidays and wondered what it might be like to celebrate with a man by her side. With Josh by her side.

No, she told herself. She could not allow herself to think of the future, to worry about what might or might not be. She needed to enjoy the present.

She needed, Meredith realized, to be more like her sister.

"What are you thinking about?" Josh asked her.

"My sister again," she said. "Wondering how she's doing."

"Mark's back by now, right?"

"Yes," Meredith said.

"So, she'll be very happy, then."

"Of course," she said, unable to keep the forced exuberance from her tone. She wanted to tell Josh the truth, to tell him that Carly was planning to break up with Mark. But then Josh would realize he had nothing to gain by entering into a venture with her. He could own Durasnow by himself and would not have to share its rights with Cartwright Enterprises.

"Don't look so worried, Meredith." Josh took her hand. "Carly's a big girl. She can take of herself."

"I'm not worried."

Why didn't she just tell Josh the truth? She wondered. She could explain why she had lied. Perhaps he would understand.

But if he didn't....the repercussions would be disastrous.

She couldn't afford to get sentimental now. There was too much at risk. Not just her heart, but her business.

"What's bothering you?" he asked, pulling into his hotel parking lot.

"I...well, I need to get back..."

"We made a deal. Twenty-four hours without business. Don't renege. It would set a very bad precedent."

She glanced over at him. It tore at her heart to think about leaving Josh now. How could she go home when she knew he was still in town? That she had thrown away precious time with him?

What would the harm be if she spent another night with him? Tomorrow they would take care of the Dura-snow contract and he would return to Europe. Then the inevitable would happen, her life would return to normal. Which meant she should enjoy every delectable moment while she still could.

"Okay," she told him. "One more night."

He led her through the hotel lobby and onto the elevator, holding her hand the whole way. Meredith leaned against him and found herself wondering once again what it would be like to be part of a real couple. Not a short-term affair, but to be with someone who would not leave at the end of the week. To be with someone who was willing to offer fidelity and loyalty. Someone who truly loved her.

"Why so quiet?" he said.

"I, uh…" She continued, verbally stumbling, "I—I feel funny not returning home. At least to get a change of clothes."

"You were right when you said you'd be hijacked into business as usual. You need a break."

She grinned.

"Go and freshen up," he said. "I've got some special plans."

"Again?" She shook her head. "I usually do all the planning."

"You take care of everyone. But who takes care of you?"

He pulled her to him and kissed her.

Ten

Josh ignored the flashing button on his phone. He knew it was his office but whatever they wanted would have to wait. He had made a deal with Meredith. He did not want to be reminded of work or commitments.

As he went over his plans for the evening, he realized that never before had he been so intent upon pleasing a woman. But he couldn't seem to help himself. He wanted to take Meredith away from her routine. He felt as if his entire self was invested in her happiness.

As Meredith bathed, he arranged for a private dinner on the hotel's enclosed rooftop terrace. Then he called the boutique downstairs and had another dress sent up. When Meredith came out of the bathroom, it was waiting for her.

She held it up and said, "Where's the rest of it?" It was a short, slinky black dress with spaghetti straps.

"I described you and they chose a dress."

"I think you might have exaggerated my qualifications a bit."

He disagreed. This was how she should be dressing, he thought. Like a princess. "Try it on," he said.

When she picked up the dress and would have headed back into the bathroom, he grabbed on to the edge of her towel. "Try it on here," he said softly.

He unraveled the towel so that she was standing in front of him completely naked. Gently he ran the towel down her long, delicate arms before bringing it back up to dab at the rivulets of moisture on her soft skin. Then he stopped and watched her.

She inhaled slightly, holding her breath, waiting for him to touch her again. He could see the hunger in her eyes. Her moist breasts glistened like satin. Her nipples were hard and erect, as if begging to be touched.

She was watching him carefully. Patiently waiting like an expectant student. A wave of possessiveness washed over him as he hooked the towel around her back. Only he had touched her so intimately. *Only he had shown her sensual pleasure.*

With a yank he pulled her into him. His lips crushed hers, devouring and consuming. She was his. Only his.

He had taught her well. She had unzipped his pants and was searching for him as she rubbed her body against him. She found him and pleasure seared through him. Her touch was intoxicating. He needed her now, needed to be inside her, to be connected to her. He lifted her up so that she was sitting on the edge of the dresser and put himself inside of her.

He was a man possessed. He kissed her lips, her hair,

her cheeks. His shirt became damp with the moisture from her still wet skin as she deepened their embrace.

He let himself go only when he felt her shudder against him. He stood still for a moment, not wanting to separate. Finally he kissed her shoulder and pulled away.

Meredith was panting but would not meet his gaze.

"Meredith?" he asked, "Are you all right?"

When she finally looked at him, he saw the tears welling in her eyes.

"I'm perfect," she said quietly.

Josh took her up to the hotel rooftop, where an ordinary roof had been transformed into a virtual Eden. Inside a heated, glass solarium was an elegant gazebo full of tropical plants flourishing despite the snow outside. Josh held her arm and led her into the gazebo where a glass table had been set for two. Dinner was waiting for them, as well as a bottle of champagne.

"Josh," she said, as he pulled out her chair for her. "Is this how you treat all your dates?"

He could tell she was pleased. "No, just you."

As he watched her close her eyes, he thought, *For once, she believes me.*

He poured the champagne and held up his glass. "Here's to the future," he said. "Our future."

Meredith smiled at the veritable feast he had arranged. Filet mignon, shrimp and a myriad of the hotel's specialties.

"You spoil me," she said. "I'll have a rough adjustment when you leave."

Josh was silent. He did not want to think about leaving but rather focus on the evening ahead. On the bewitching woman sitting across from him.

"What are you thinking about?" she asked.

He wanted to ask about the tears she'd shed after they had made love. But he felt his question might make her shut down again. So instead he answered, "I'm thinking that you made it. One whole day without any communication with the office."

"You, too."

"I have the feeling it's a bigger accomplishment for you than for me."

"It didn't seem that difficult," she said. "I was distracted. It's hard to believe tomorrow I return to life as usual." She glanced downward and for a moment it looked as if she might cry.

He could not bear to see her sad. No more than he could bear the thought of leaving her behind. "What about a bigger distraction?"

"What do you mean?" she asked.

"Come back with me, Meredith," he said, surprised to hear himself speak the words. But he had been thinking about it all day. She had gotten Durasnow, had saved her company. She was entitled to some time off.

But his real reason for wanting her to leave with him was selfishly motivated. He did not want to go home without her.

"I want you to come to Europe with me," he told her. "I want to show you my life. No...I want to share my life with you."

"What are you saying?"

Tell her. Tell her what you're feeling. Tell her what you've known since you made love on Bear Mountain. "I'm in love with you," he said.

She shook her head. "This is just an affair...you have lots of women..."

"No," he said adamantly. "What I feel for you...it's different. I've been single a long time. And now I know why. I've been waiting, Meredith. Waiting for you."

Meredith felt her world come to a crashing halt. She couldn't believe what Josh was saying, She'd been certain that Josh was incapable of love, that his interest in her was purely sexual.

"Josh, I haven't been honest with you."

"What do you mean?"

She swallowed. *Just tell him. Tell him and get it over with.* "Last night...I came to see you because I knew Carly was planning to break up with Mark."

Josh leaned back in his chair, a stunned expression on his face.

"I knew that I had to get an agreement with you before you found out. Because once she broke up with him..."

"I would have no reason to agree to sharing the rights to Durasnow with you." His eyes looked dark and empty. His face was void of expression.

"I'm sorry," she managed to admit. "I knew I could never match your money. You were right. My only hold over the Durans was Carly."

"I see." His voice was cold, completely different from the warm, loving tone he had used only moments earlier. "So you did what you had to do to ensure getting the rights."

She glanced away. "I never meant for things to happen the way they did."

"No?" He threw down his napkin. Standing, he walked to the side of the solarium and looked out at the city of Aspen, lit up in front of him. "That's the second time I've heard you say that."

Meredith couldn't bear to look at him. The sound of his voice was enough to break her heart.

"I'm sorry," she said.

Josh turned around and looked at her. "Not half as sorry as I am."

Eleven

"So I suppose this means both of you will be home for Christmas this year?'' her mother asked Meredith the following morning. Both she and Carly were sitting at the dining room table with their mother. Neither sister appeared well rested.

Meredith had arrived home from Josh's the previous evening, hoping to escape into her room unseen, but had been stopped just as she was closing the door by her tearful mother. Viera had informed her about what Meredith had already known: Carly had broken off her engagement.

Meredith looked around the table. If appearances were any indication, *none* of them had gotten much sleep. Viera's eyes were red and swollen. Carly's usual healthy, bright face was pale.

Meredith knew she didn't look any better. She had

been unable to sleep, haunted by thoughts of Josh. She couldn't stop thinking about him. How could he have said he was in love with her? How could she believe him?

What difference did it make now anyway? Their relationship was over. She had truly hurt him and they would never be together again.

Meredith looked at Carly and realized she should be worrying about her sister, not herself. Carly had lost her fiancé.

Viera cleared her throat and Meredith realized that her mother was still waiting for an answer. "I guess I'll be home for Christmas," she said.

"Well," her mother replied, "I suppose I have to change my plans. I can't very well leave you both alone."

"Mother," Carly said, "we're perfectly capable of taking care of ourselves."

"I beg to differ," Viera said. "Just look at the mess we're in now."

Meredith didn't need to be reminded. There were many things to take care of. The company's stock would spiral downward once word leaked out they had lost Durasnow. Meredith would almost certainly be fired. The impact on her family's life would be tremendous. The house would need to be sold, finances cut severely.

"I'm sorry," Meredith said.

When Viera left the room, Meredith glanced at her sister.

"You should've seen Mark's face," Carly said, crossing her arm over her forehead. "He looked so sad when I told him I was calling off the wedding."

"You did the right thing," Meredith said. "You can't marry someone you don't love."

"But that's the odd thing," Carly said. "I think I do love him."

"What?"

"Well, now the pressure is off and I can finally think. And I'm thinking that maybe I really do love Mark."

"Oh, Carly," Meredith said. She was glad her sister had finally realized the truth, but she was worried she might have realized it too late.

"What about you?" Carly asked.

"What do you mean?"

"How do you feel about Josh now that it's all over?"

"I'm disappointed, naturally. I had looked forward to sharing Durasnow with him."

"But that's all?"

"Our relationship," she said, straightening, "was totally based on business."

"So there's no problem," Carly said suspiciously.

"No problem at all."

"None," said Meredith. She stood. "If you'll excuse me, I should be getting back to the office."

There was no problem. Except for the mind-numbing pain that surrounded her, except for crying every time she thought of Josh, nothing was wrong.

She forced a smile. "It's nothing a little work won't cure."

Josh couldn't sleep. It had felt strange to be in the same bed that he had made love to Meredith in only hours earlier. He kept reaching out, expecting her to be beside him.

How could he have been so blind? He had actually

believed Meredith cared about him, actually believed that perhaps they'd had something worth fighting for. But he had been mistaken. Meredith had had little interest in pursuing a relationship with him. It had all been about business, pure and simple. She had been using him.

And he had allowed it to happen. He had bought her story, lock, stock, and barrel.

He walked around the hotel room, anxiously pacing. He glanced out the window at Bear Mountain, the place where they had first made love.

And as he remembered the tears in her eyes during the last time they made love he realized Meredith was trapped in her own private ice castle. A part of her was still alive, fighting to be let out. Fighting to care.

Could he help her? Should he?

After all, Meredith had been right. They had only spent two nights together. That was hardly enough time to form a deep, lasting relationship.

But never before had a woman made him feel so alive. Never before had a woman challenged him so. For the first time in his life he had met someone with whom he could look forward to spending the rest of his days. A woman he would never tire of.

A woman he could love.

And that was the problem. *He loved her.*

He had no choice. Meredith wanted Durasnow. And he was going to get it for her.

Meredith had suffered another terrible night and the day didn't look much better. She had already found two runs in her stockings, her car had refused to start and a cab had rushed past her, spraying her with muddy ice water.

When she'd arrived at work she'd found her once boisterous office somber and quiet. The few people involved in the Durasnow pitch had been sworn to silence, which guaranteed the whole office knew. Cartwright had received a blow from which it might not recover. Durasnow was lost. She had heard that Josh had been awarded the rights that morning. Cartwright Enterprises may not have to declare bankruptcy yet, but a reorganization was almost certain.

Her office door opened. Carly walked in, Viera marching behind her. Meredith stood. "What are you both doing here?" Meredith had returned to Denver the day before. As far as she knew, her mother and sister had planned to stay in Aspen.

"Your sister has news," Viera said.

"I'm married."

"You're...you're what?" Meredith sat down.

"Mark and I were married today. Less than an hour ago," Carly told her.

"I flew into town last night and surprised him. We ran over to the courthouse at lunch."

"But...but..."

"I know!" Viera exclaimed. She dropped into the chair as if exhausted. "Why couldn't she have gotten married when she was supposed to?"

Carly ignored her mother. "I'm so sorry, Meredith. I made you lose Durasnow...I screwed everything up..."

"No," Meredith said. Her head was spinning. "I just...I don't understand."

"Once Durasnow was sold, there was absolutely no business reason for me to marry Mark. And once that pressure was gone...I just realized how much I loved him. I mean, I always did. I just wanted to marry him for love, not because it made business sense.''

''I see.''

''And now we have a wedding without a bride and groom,'' Viera said. ''How embarrassing.''

''Oh, Mother,'' Meredith said. ''Calm down.'' She stood and walked over to kiss her sister on the cheek. ''I'm happy for you.''

Carly smiled. ''What about you?''

Meredith returned to her desk and busied herself with a stack of papers. ''I'm preparing my resignation.''

''Oh, Meredith,'' Carly said.

''It's all right. It's the only way. I gambled and lost.''

''But you're the best thing that ever happened to this company!'' Viera said.

''Says my mother. But I can guarantee the board's opinion is going to differ.''

''Maybe if you called Josh and talked to him...'' Carly said.

''No,'' Meredith said. ''Absolutely not.''

''Why not?'' Carly said. ''You could talk to him, convince him to share the rights. If anyone can persuade him, it's you.''

''That's where you're wrong. Anyone *but* me could persuade him at this point.''

Just then her assistant walked into the room and placed a small box on her desk. ''This just arrived for you.''

Meredith unwrapped the brown paper package to find a perfectly round synthetic snowball. She picked up the note tucked alongside and felt her knees grow weak as she read it.

"What's wrong?" Carly exclaimed.

"It's from Josh," she said finally. "He's signed over the rights to Durasnow."

Meredith read the note again, as if a secret meaning might pop out at her. But it was as direct as could be.

I'm giving you Durasnow. Congratulations, Meredith.
You were right. You always win.
                         Josh

Meredith sat down. Carly and her mother hugged each other. "This is wonderful," Carly said. "Now you don't have to resign."

But Meredith didn't feel wonderful. She felt terrible. She had won the rights, but suddenly it didn't matter. What mattered was that she had lost Josh.

"I don't deserve this," Meredith said.

"Who cares whether—" Viera began.

"I care. And I care what Josh thinks." Meredith shook her head and looked around her office. "This just doesn't seem important anymore."

"You love him!" Carly exclaimed joyfully. "You really do."

"Go after him," Carly said. "I have Josh's address in Switzerland. Even if he's already left Denver, he won't beat you back there by much."

Meredith didn't need any more convincing. She grabbed her purse. With a quick hug and a kiss goodbye, she was off.

As Meredith disappeared down the hall, Viera turned toward Carly and smiled. "Perhaps," she said, "I won't cancel the wedding just yet."

Twelve

Josh arrived at the Zurich airport in a dangerous mood. Mechanical problems in Denver had forced him to take a later flight and transfer out of Baltimore, adding another four hours to his already long trip. It was now nearly midnight.

He grabbed his bags and headed outside. This had been the trip from hell.

As he climbed into a taxi, his thoughts focused again on the woman he had left behind. He wondered how Meredith had felt when she'd received word that he had given her Durasnow. He had no doubt that she had been relieved, probably very surprised. But there would have been no regret. No what-ifs. That would be his burden.

As the taxi drove through the small, narrow cobblestone streets, a light snow began to fall. It looked like a scene out of a fairy tale: narrow, old buildings side by side, Christmas lights twinkling in the windows, comforting puffs of smoke pouring out of the chimneys. He could almost imagine the families inside. Children playing around the Christmas tree, their parents enjoying the warmth of family togetherness.

How he had wanted to bring Meredith here. How he would have loved to have shown her Switzerland. To have welcomed her into his life.

The cab pulled up in front of his house. It had originally been a bank, so the outside still looked like a place of business. He had little time to make the changes he had always planned. Nor did he have much inclination. He had been waiting, he realized, for that special person. That special woman who would help him turn his house into a home.

He paid the driver and grabbed his bags, walked up to his front door and turned the lock. And stopped.

He saw her out of the corner of his eye. She stepped out of the shadows, like a ghost or a figment of his imagination.

Meredith.

Snow coated her eyelashes and hair. Her cheeks were red from the cold. "What are you doing here?" he asked, stunned.

"Why did you do it, Josh?" she asked. "Why did you give me Durasnow?" Meredith was not acting like a woman who had won a business deal. She seemed almost defeated. Fragile. The change was alarming.

"Because," he said, "I know how much it meant to you. You've put so much of yourself into that company."

"Thank you," she said. "It was generous of you and

I'm grateful. But how can I possibly accept a multi-million dollar gift?''

''You and I both know your company will not survive without Durasnow.''

She winced as if his words held daggers.

He realized the effect his comment had upon her and softened his tone. ''I couldn't imagine what losing that company would do to you. I wasn't about to let it go under.''

''You let me win, but winning doesn't matter to me anymore.'' Her eyes were big and full of tears. ''I should've told you how I felt the other night instead of acting like such a fool. I care about you. I always have. My family knew that. That's why they concocted that ridiculous scheme about me having to distract you from Carly. As soon as the helicopter dropped us off on that mountain, I knew I was in over my head. I tried to distract myself with business but it didn't help. One of the reasons I was so anxious to get back down that mountain was because I was afraid of you. Afraid of what I was feeling.''

''And what was that?'' he asked softly.

''Love,'' she said, her voice a whisper. ''I told myself that my time with you was all about clinching the deal, but that wasn't true. I stayed because I couldn't bring myself to leave. I stayed because I wanted to be with you.'' She focused her eyes on him and said, ''I lied not only to you but to myself.''

They were surrounded by such overwhelming quiet one could practically hear the snow as it fell.

''You were frightened?''

She nodded. ''I was scared of getting hurt. But being

with you is not nearly as terrifying as the idea of being without you."

He could not stand to see her in pain. He took her hand and held it. "I'm not going to hurt you."

"I'm not asking you to make a promise you can't keep."

"You don't understand," he said, lifting her chin so that she was looking at him. "This isn't about making a promise. It's about what I want. And I want you." He kissed her tenderly and intimately, his lips searing against hers. He didn't care what it took nor how long. He would prove his love. "Marry me, Princess."

"Oh, Josh," she murmured as his demanding lips grazed her neck. She pulled back for a moment. As she tenderly caressed his face she looked into his eyes and said the words that he longed to hear: "I love you."

With their kiss, they seemed to melt into each other. Then he opened the door. "Come inside where it's warm."

Shortly before Christmas, three hundred people crowded into the Rosewood ballroom to witness the marriage of the biggest playboy Aspen had ever seen, to one of the most influential women in the country. The affair was even more elaborate than predicted. Viera turned the ballroom into an ornate winter forest. Giant evergreen trees sparkled and thousands of white roses peeked out of mounds of Durasnow. A midnight-blue, tentlike roof mimicked the night sky.

Ever since Carly had announced her elopement and Meredith her engagement, high society had been in an uproar. Everyone was surprised to learn that although the Cartwright wedding was happening as planned, the participants were not exactly the ones mentioned on the invitation. Some claimed Meredith only got engaged when the Rosewood wouldn't refund her deposit for her sister's wedding; others said her reasons were more personal, whispering about a "need" to get married and of a "shotgun" affair.

But when Meredith appeared wearing a skintight, white designer gown studded with crystals, the gossips were silenced. Everyone agreed they had never seen a more radiant or beautiful bride. And there was no mistaking the look in her eyes as she walked toward her handsome fiancé. It was obvious that it was neither a child nor frugality that motivated her to walk down the aisle. It was love.

Meredith was so excited she did not notice the hubbub around her. All she could think about was Josh and their future together. She had imagined this moment many times, but it was always with dread. How could she marry knowing the travails that awaited? But she no longer worried about the Cartwright curse. She and Josh were meant for one another. Their hearts had already been united. Their wedding was simply a celebration of their passion for each other.

They said their vows standing side by side. As Josh promised to love her forever, her heart swelled. He caught her eye and pulled back her veil. In a spontaneous moment that the gossips would mention for years, he kissed her passionately, not even waiting for the minister's permission.

After the wedding, the guests sat at the satin-covered banquet tables to enjoy cracked lobsters and champagne. Meredith looped her arm through Josh's and cheerfully made the rounds, welcoming guests. When she saw

Carly talking business on her cell phone, doing business in the midst of this glamorous wedding, she laughed. Not long ago, that was me, she thought.

The past few weeks had been a whirlwind of activity. She and Carly had traded roles, with Carly taking the helm of the business as Meredith devoted herself to her wedding. In the process, her unreliable sister had been transformed into a business executive. And the change seemed to have worked wonders for Carly's marriage. It was obvious from the loving way Mark regarded his new bride that he could not have been prouder.

"Meredith!" Carly exclaimed, hanging up the phone and giving her sister a hug. "Are you having fun?"

But before Meredith could answer, they were interrupted by Carly's cell phone. Carly glanced at the number and said, "Again?" She flipped open the phone and mouthed to Meredith, "Sorry."

Meredith watched as Carly walked away, immersed in business.

Josh kissed Meredith's shoulder. "What are you thinking about, Princess?"

"Carly. She hasn't even had a chance to enjoy the wedding. She's too busy with work."

He slowly and softly brushed the back of his hand down her cheek and said, "You can always go back to Cartwright if you miss it."

She shook her head. "Not a chance." It was time to leave. After a European honeymoon, she and Josh were going into business together. Their first project: the Algiers Hotel. They planned to redo the entire top floor as living quarters, turning it into a cozy home. "It's Carly's turn now." She squeezed his hand and said, "I'm ready for a new adventure."

Josh smiled. "Then follow me."

They made their way through the crowd of well-wishers. Josh took off his coat and wrapped it around Meredith's shoulders as they slipped outside. Meredith was thrilled to see that it was snowing.

"I have an early Christmas present for you," he whispered. He reached into the pocket of the suit coat she was wearing and pulled out a small gift-wrapped box.

She unwrapped the silver paper. Inside was a tiny diamond crown on a platinum chain.

He took the necklace and fastened it around her neck. "A crown fit for a princess."

As he said her nickname, she felt something stir deep within her. Princess. That was exactly how he made her feel. The name which had once signified a condition of isolation and pain now meant just the opposite.

He slid his arm around her waist and turned her toward him. She wrapped her hands around his neck and gave him a kiss that proved the ice princess had finally melted. And all it took was love.

* * * * *

Look for Margaret Allison's next book
for Silhouette Desire,
A SINGLE DEMAND,
available February 2005.

Silhouette

Desire

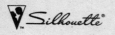

INTIMATE MOMENTS™

presents the continuing saga of the
crime-fighting McCall family

by favorite author

Maggie Price

Where peril and
passion collide.

*Available in
December 2004:*

Shattered Vows

(Intimate Moments #1335)

Lieutenant Brandon McCall is facing his toughest
assignment yet—to protect his estranged wife from
an escaped killer. But when the investigation forces
Brandon and Tory into close quarters, old passions are
revived—and new dangers threaten to destroy them.

*Look for the next book in this exciting miniseries, coming
in June 2005 to Silhouette Bombshell:*

TRIGGER EFFECT (#48)

Available at your favorite retail outlet.

COMING NEXT MONTH

#1621 SHOCKING THE SENATOR—Leanne Banks
Dynasties: The Danforths
Abraham Danforth had tried to deny his attraction to his campaign manager, Nicola Granville, for months—although they *had* shared a secret night of passion. With the election won and Abraham becoming Georgia's new senator, would the child Nicola now carried become the scandal that would ruin his career?

#1622 WILD IN THE MOMENT—Jennifer Greene
The Scent of Lavender
The whirring blizzard, the cracking fire and their intimate quarters had Daisy Campbell and Teague Larson unexpectedly sharing a wild moment. The two hardly seemed like a match made in heaven...so why couldn't Daisy turn down Teague's surprise business deal and *many more* wild moments?

#1623 THE ICE MAIDEN'S SHEIKH—Alexandra Sellers
Sons of the Desert
Beauty Jalia Shahbazi had been a princess-under-wraps for twenty-seven years and that was how she planned to keep it. That was until sexy Sheikh Latif Al Razzaqi Shahin awakened her Middle Eastern roots... and her passion. But Latif wanted to lay claim to more than Jalia's body— and she dared not offer more. .

#1624 FORBIDDEN PASSION—Emilie Rose
Lynn Riggan's brother-in-law Sawyer was everything her recently deceased husband was not: caring, giving and loving. The last thing Lynn was looking for was forbidden passion, but after briefly giving in to their intense mutual attraction, she couldn't get Sawyer out of her head... or her heart. Might an unexpected arrival give her all she'd ever wanted?

#1625 RIDING THE STORM—Brenda Jackson
Jayla Coles had met many Mr. Wrongs when she finally settled on visiting the sperm bank to get what she wanted. Then she met the perfect storm— fire captain Storm Westmoreland. They planned on a no-strings-attached affair, but their brief encounter left them with more than just lasting memories....

#1626 THE SEDUCTION REQUEST—Michelle Celmer
Millionaire restaurateur Matt Conway returned to his hometown to prove he'd attained ultimate success. But when he ran into former best friend and lover, Emily Douglas, winning over her affection became his number-one priority. Problem was, she was planning on marrying another man...and Matt was just the guy to make her change her mind.

SDCNM1104